W9-ART-524

PETER EDWARDS

the Biker's Brother

a novel

annick press
toronto + berkeley

RAP

3 2401 00928 606 5

© 2017 Peter Edwards

Cover art/design by Kong Njo
Edited by Lorissa Sengara
Designed by Kong Njo

Annick Press Ltd.

All rights reserved. No part of this work covered by the copyrights hereon may be reproduced or used in any form or by any means—graphic, electronic, or mechanical—without the prior written permission of the publisher.

We acknowledge the support of the Canada Council for the Arts and the Ontario Arts Council, and the participation of the Government of Canada/la participation du gouvernement du Canada for our publishing activities.

Canada

ONTARIO ARTS COUNCIL
CONSEIL DES ARTS DE L'ONTARIO
an Ontario government agency
un organisme du gouvernement de l'Ontario

Cataloging in Publication

Edwards, Peter, 1956-, author
     The biker's brother / Peter Edwards.

Issued in print and electronic formats.
ISBN 978-1-55451-936-1 (hardcover).–ISBN 978-1-55451-935-4 (softcover).–
ISBN 978-1-55451-937-8 (EPUB).–ISBN 978-1-55451-938-5 (PDF)

     I. Title.

PS8609.D864B55 2017   jC813'.6   C2017-901683-0
                                               C2017-901684-9

Cover photos: Motorbike © iStockphoto.com/visual7;
young man © iStockphoto.com/dcdp

Published in the U.S.A. by Annick Press (U.S.) Ltd.
Distributed in Canada by University of Toronto Press.
Distributed in the U.S.A. by Publishers Group West.

Printed in Canada

Visit us at: www.annickpress.com
Visit Peter Edwards at http://peteredwardsauthor.com/

Also available in e-book format. Please visit www.annickpress.com/
ebooks.html for more details. Or scan

To my parents, Ken and Winona Edwards,
for letting me dream big

—P.E.

*"My barn having burned down,
I can now see the moon."*

—Mizuta Masahide,
seventeenth-century Japanese poet and samurai

Brenda's standing near the roadway. There are those eyes again, those soft bunny rabbit eyes, but this time, she's pale and trembling and scared. She looks like she's in shock. I can see she's been crying. A lot.

All the action's centered on the garage.

A Volvo SUV with a sign reading "CORONER, Dr. Edward James" in the back window pulls up by the police command post. A man of about sixty with a shock of graying hair steps out. His glasses are perched at the end of his nose and his hair is trimmed in a brush cut, only higher.

"Dr. James," one of the cops says, and leads him toward the garage.

He's calm enough. I imagine he's been to plenty of nasty crime and accident scenes. It's time to go, before the attention shifts from him to me.

As I press on the gas pedal, another police car pulls up, and Brenda gets in the back. For an instant, she's alongside me. I've thought of her almost nonstop since the party, but I never once imagined the lost expression I see on her face.

Her eyes meet mine and she mouths some words. I can make them out clearly even though I can't hear her. They couldn't hit me harder if she was screaming them out loud.

"He's dead."

Chapter

1

She is standing there under the Confederate flag looking like a goddess, between the tub of beer on ice and the meth whore. The band attacks some old song that might be the Rolling Stones or might be Lynyrd Skynyrd or might be an original, previously unheard composition. What they don't destroy with their musicianship is finished off by their amplifiers, which mush any surviving clean notes into a nasty, unrecognizable pulp.

Happy hillbillies stomp about the barn floor in a white-trash semblance of dancing. It's not clear if they're actually dancing or just making fun of the whole idea of dancing, or a bit of both. Heavy boots, a lack of natural rhythm, a poor band, and undanceable tunes conspire to make them look like zombies on a hot plate.

"Mankind has evolved to this?" I say.

It's as good a line as I'm capable of, and she smiles in a conspiratorial way that makes it easy for me to ask my second question.

"Want to dance?"

I know she'll say yes. Girls who say no don't come to these parties.

"Josh Williams?" she says.

I nod. She remembers my name. We're off to a promising start.

I definitely remember her name: Brenda Wallace. Brenda reminds me of a teenage Scarlett Johansson, but a taller, leaner version. Brenda's somehow beautiful without really trying, graceful even when she's standing still. Today, she's super-feminine in loose-fitting Levi's red-tab jeans and a white denim shirt with shiny snaps and the sleeves cut off. She has no visible tattoos, and no piercings that I can see, and her hair appears to be its natural blond. In a barn full of people making gimmicky, clichéd personal statements, her big thing seems to be having no gimmick at all.

Her eyes are the exception. Her makeup is dark and exaggerated and somehow leaves the impression of what happens when a little girl experiments in front of a mirror with Mommy's eye shadow and mascara, imagining she's all grown up. Her eyes look just the way I remember them: mysterious, but also soft and bright and reminding me of a bunny rabbit.

She's probably a little bit older than me, but not

much. A girl half as hot could intimidate me under normal conditions with her looks alone, but not today. Somehow today feels special.

It's perfect July weather: not too hot but clearly summer—just right for an afternoon barbecue, especially now that she's here. It's the first time I've seen her in months.

Brenda appeared last September in the halls of our school, but we didn't have any classes together and she vanished halfway through the year, when I hadn't advanced past the smiling-at-her-in-the-halls stage. We didn't have any friends in common. I don't actually recall her having any close friends at all, or belonging to any clubs or teams. But now we're the only teenagers at the party, and it seems natural that we finally talk.

Brenda doesn't really fit in here—she's younger and prettier and not as worn-down as the other women hanging around—but she owns the room anyway. Her expression is one of curiosity if not surprise, somehow combining sweetness with adult intelligence.

"What brings you here?" I ask, swigging from a Coke.

"A Harley," she replies.

Beautiful and witty, though not entirely original. Definitely sassy. If this isn't love, it's dangerously close. Is there any better proof of the existence of God than having a hot girl joke with you and not needing to fake a laugh?

Out of the corner of my eye, I can see Billy Davis through the open barn doorway. He's just getting off of his bike. Billy's the only black guy here, which isn't that odd since there just aren't many black people in our town. His nephew Cal plays football with me; he's a pretty good running back and a nice guy. Billy's smiling as he surveys the scene.

That smile transforms into a look of alarm as he sees a club member named Trollop walking fast toward him with a younger biker named Wally at his side. I can tell by Trollop's gait that he's upset about something.

Trollop's in his early fifties and he likes to gives off an aura of power, as though he could take down anyone in the club. He might have been tough back in the day, but that day is long past, if it ever existed at all. He has long, scraggly white hair that he likes to pull back in a ponytail, when he's cleaning up. He's not skinny but he's definitely not heavily muscled. I'm sure lots of people at the party could tune him up in a couple of minutes, but there's still something nasty and dangerous about him.

Billy barely gets the word "bro" out of his mouth before Trollop catches him hard on the side of the face with a fist. It's a clear sucker punch. Billy freezes. He doesn't even attempt to defend himself, just crumples by the doorway as Trollop proceeds to put the boots to him. Wally stands nearby, just in case Billy somehow miraculously gets up and starts to rally.

Billy curls into a fetal position as Trollop gives him one last kick that's mostly for show. Then he looks over at a guy I've never seen before, a huge biker from the Popeyes Motorcycle Club who's wearing a red vest. The Popeye gives a slight nod and Trollop responds with a smirk.

"Better not come back," Trollop says as he walks away from Billy and back into the barn.

Chapter 2

I t all happens so quickly, probably less than a minute from start to finish. Fights aren't that remarkable in my brother's world. And this party, this biker club—it's my brother's world. And here, you can punch a man at 9:00 p.m., hug him and have another beer with him at 10:00 p.m., and then punch him again, repeating the cycle for as long as your energy and beer and knuckles hold out.

Today, though, something feels different. This thing with Trollop wasn't a joke or someone just acting tough. It feels like something big's about to happen, like something's about to snap. Maybe it has to do with the Popeyes. It's the first time I've seen them at a party, not that I go to all of them. The Annihilators, the local club my brother belongs to, love to throw punches and act tough, but the Popeyes are from the big city, and have a reputation for pulling triggers and planting bombs and burning places down. They also have some pretty strict rules: I've heard that some of the big clubs don't allow black bikers to join, or even attend their parties. Is that what I just witnessed with Billy? I can't see my brother, Jamie, being comfortable with that.

Whatever just happened, no one's dead and it doesn't seem to have fazed Brenda. She's lost in her dancing, exaggerating her movements and facial expressions in a jerky-but-almost-graceful brave way I love but don't really understand. There's something exposed and magical in how she dances, and I'd rather think about it than whatever is going on with Trollop. She seems so far away, and then she looks me straight in the eyes and holds my gaze like she can see right inside me, and I couldn't possibly feel closer to her. Whatever she's dancing to, it's coming from inside her head, not the band. Their music's from a different generation, though that's fitting since the Annihilators are like something out of a time warp. Don't hold your breath waiting for any Kendrick Lamar, Calvin Harris, G-Eazy, or Drake here.

I hear a Harley start up and I assume it's Billy Davis riding away.

From across the barn, Jamie looks over in my direction. He's chatting with a husky, scruffy Popeye who looks like he's spent some time in the gym. Jamie gestures for me to come over. Brenda sees this and grins.

As I make my way toward my brother, I see that Brenda is following me. It's insane what a rush that gives me—to have this great girl at my side, like we're together. I wonder if Jamie can see how stoked I am. I glance over at him, trying to send a secret brother-code signal for "Dude, check this out," but he's not paying attention. Someone else is, though. Perched on a stool not far from my brother is Carlito, a young member of the Annihilators. He's in his early twenties, somewhere between my age and Jamie's. With his sharp features and brooding expression, he looks a little like a young Al Pacino—unoriginally, his nickname comes from an ancient Pacino movie that I've never seen. His self-styled trademark is his black lizard cowboy boots, tipped with silver on the toes and heels. He's watching us as we walk across the room—and he isn't smiling.

I try to ignore him as I make the introductions.

"Jamie, this is Brenda."

It seems inadequate, given how I'm feeling, but I don't know how else to introduce her. She's relaxed, though, and there's no awkward silence.

"Hi, Brenda. Pleased to meet you."

Jamie's jet-black hair is longer than mine, and he always has what looks to be a three-day scruff of beard. His smile is broad and genuine and stays on his face as he welcomes her.

"I'm Trent's sister," Brenda says.

Jamie's face goes a little tight for a second before

he forces a smile and nods his head, then turns toward his friend.

"This is Tom from Quebec."

Tom gives me a biker handshake, our thumbs interlocked.

"Tom played football. He tells me he was pretty good."

Tom rolls his eyes and grins at the little joke.

Jamie loves to introduce me as a football player. He was okay himself when he was my age.

"Shouldn't you be rehabbing instead of dancing?" he says, turning back to me.

He's talking about my knee, though it's pretty much a hundred percent now. I can hear just a hint of the old stammer in his voice; these days, he typically speaks in little spurts so that you can hardly notice it. His mumbly growl might make him sound tough, but I know the stammer's still there. I bet a lot of his biker buddies don't.

"And really, you call that dancing?" Jamie adds. "Don't make me go out there and show you how it's done."

He's facing Brenda now, smiling. She's clearly enjoying the moment too. It's all polite, not flirty.

"Don't mean to keep you from better things," Jamie says, still looking at Brenda.

"You couldn't if you tried," I reply.

Jamie and I smile at each other, and Brenda blushes a little.

"My big brother," I tell her as we walk away.

"Bro?" she asks. The sarcastic edge is back in her voice.

"Biological bro."

She appreciates the distinction and beams in a way that pulls me closer. Her smiles are addictive. There are plenty of worse things in this barn to get addicted to.

"I kinda figured that out," she says. "He looks like you."

Something in her expression suggests that's a compliment. I'm more buff and less tattooed than Jamie, but I suppose there is a resemblance. Mom likes to say that my toddler pictures are almost identical to his, and that even she has trouble telling them apart sometimes.

"He wishes," I reply, smirking.

"There's my brother, Trent, over there." Brenda gestures to a weedy-looking guy over by the beer tub.

I knew already. I've heard a bit about him. He's the club's cook—specializing in methamphetamine, not food. Even though I'm not in the club, it's pretty common knowledge. Jamie hates that the Annihilators are now involved in that stuff. I wonder if Brenda sees me flinch a little at the mention of his name. If so, she doesn't let on.

"I'm staying with him," she says. "For a while."

She's not smiling now.

Chapter
3

I think Brenda's about to tell me more, but she just dances on. Instead of talking about Trent, she gestures toward Trollop and some other bikers, including Wally Parkinson, the guy who backed Trollop up when he attacked Billy Davis.

"All that's missing is the circus music," Brenda says.

Wally's a meth-head, so no surprise that he's just staring vacantly in the direction of the band. He's from nearby Stratford, famed for its theater festival, and is wearing a T-shirt with a picture of a fuzzy-eyed Shakespeare and the slogan "Stratford: Come for the Macbeth and stay for the meth." Wally's not a full member of the Annihilators, although I'm sure he'd love to be. Anything above the level of public nuisance would be an upgrade for Wally.

Now Trollop's undoing his club vest to show Wally *his* T-shirt, which bears a cartoon image of a dead rat lying on its back with its feet in the air and *X*s over its eyes. Around the dead rodent is a big red circle with a red line through it, and underneath are the words "Rats Must Be Exterminated." The back of the shirt reads, "Progress is made one funeral at a time." Talking with Wally is a biker called Tiny who tips the Toledos at well over 350 pounds and is wearing a tight T-shirt with the slogan "I beat anorexia."

Not far from them are the "old ladies," the wives or steady girlfriends of club members. The most eye-catching of the group is a hot blonde whose boobs are so big and firm you could comfortably land a small plane on them. She's dressed like one of those models you see on calendars in ancient auto body shops, but she's not as young or as hot. Still, I'm betting most of the guys on the football team would happily attempt a hookup, but she's totally untouchable. Her husband is a full patch member of the Spartans, a biker club from London, one town over. He has a shaved head, a nasty prison record, and a lightning bolt patch on the front of his vest, indicating that he's killed for the club. He also has a teardrop tattooed under one eye, another not-so-subtle announcement that he's taken a life. You don't see him around much, and today he seems more interested in the Popeyes than the Annihilators. The Spartans have an on-again, off-again relationship with the Annihilators, so it's interesting to see any of them here today at all.

The old ladies keep an eye on a half dozen or so splashers, the current term for unattached women at the bottom of the social order who like to party particularly hard. Today, they're writhing to the music, as if it really were danceable and even hypnotic.

The splashers are an eager-to-please bunch, and the old ladies worry that they might steal away their men or at least infect them with some nasty disease. I don't say this from much experience, just observation. They make you want to run from them and laugh at them and use them and warn them and protect them, all at the same time.

A splasher staggers by wearing tight jeans accessorized by a "YIELD" sign on her chest and a "STOP" sign on her back and nothing in between. You might think this would be sexy but you'd be wrong.

She's clearly stoned, and I wonder if she'll remember any of this tomorrow. The creepiest part of the whole sick mess is Trollop cackling away at the sight of her, looking somehow triumphant and expectant.

Brenda is immediately at her side, quietly offering comfort and support with an arm around the woman's waist. She doesn't pause to look at me, or her brother, for direction or approval.

An old biker named Ripper smiles gently and steps in. With his gray ponytail and full beard, Ripper looks like a warrior version of Santa. He leads the splasher away to a kitchen area, where he directs some old ladies to take care of her. Trollop gives them a dirty look that turns into a smirk as he resumes chatting with his friends.

Brenda had just started dancing with me again, as if what just happened is no big deal, when a voice rings out across the barn.

"Little bro!"

That's Trollop, addressing me—I'm the only one who gets called "little bro" around here. He seems particularly proud of himself since he put the boots to Billy in front of the Popeye from Quebec. He has a cell phone in each hand, as though he's too busy and complex a man for just one phone, or one universe. He's carrying a beer too, pinning the can against his ribs with an elbow.

I'm trying to think of a clever comeback, but it doesn't matter. Trollop has no intention of stopping to chat; he's already swaggered past me and is on his way toward Carlito and a couple of other Annihilators, with Wally and Tiny close behind. I watch them talk: as a non-member, I can't just barge into that conversation without some sort of invitation, even if I wanted to—and I don't.

Carlito's watching us again. I'm not sure if he's smiling or smirking but there's something about him I just don't like. I know he went to my school before I got there, although I've never heard of him distinguishing himself in sports, or in anything else for that matter.

I'm pretty sure I could take Carlito in a fair fight, but his reputation is for guns and knives and gang attacks, not fairness. Still, the way Brenda looks back at him suggests they have some shared history. The thought makes my stomach clench. I've never felt jealous of him until right now. Maybe he senses that I'm watching him back because he smiles and nods at me as if I'm a eunuch or her gay dance partner or the warm-up act before he takes over.

Brenda picks up on the silent drama and spins around so her back is toward him, then steps up the pace. She puts no pressure on me to keep up with her, which is a good thing, since dancing isn't my best event. Carlito turns away too, drifting over to a pack of other full patch members. It's as if they have adult business to attend to and are content to leave the dancing to us kids.

There are a couple of particularly large bikers at the barn today who I know are members of the Popeyes. They don't look relaxed, or like they even want to be relaxed. The Popeyes are an international club, with chapters on four continents. In contrast, next to no one knows the Annihilators exist once you get outside of our area code. The Popeyes appear to be checking things out today, not partying. A few are wearing red Kevlar vests that look new and a bit bulky, something like the ones police SWAT teams wear. These guys seem particularly keyed up. None of the Annihilators are into Kevlar vests; I imagine they'd find them heavy and sweaty and expensive—though I could see Trollop getting one just to look dangerous. He's a bit in awe of the Popeyes, although he's trying not to show it. Ripper's harder to read.

One of the Popeyes says something to Brenda's brother, Trent, and his face tightens up. This guy looks jacked up on steroids, something I recognize from my gym. I've been told he's a Quebecer from the Nomads. The Nomads are an elite chapter of the Popeyes; these guys travel anywhere they want and pull rank on pretty well anyone in the club. You don't see Nomads often, and when you do, no one is all that comfortable. What's particularly unsettling about this man are his eyes. They're hard like bullets, and I feel like they're staring right at me. Then he puts on a frozen smile as Trollop shuffles in to take a selfie of them together with one of his phones.

Jamie walks by carrying beers for Ripper and himself, but nothing for Trent, who's standing nearby. Trent says something to Jamie that I can't hear, and Jamie turns back at him and glares. And that's all it takes.

"I'm not your waiter," Jamie says.

I'm surprised by Jamie's tone, but not shocked. I've seen this before, when he's close to snapping. If Trent's smart, he'll notice that Jamie's body is tensing up, like a dog just before it lunges. When Jamie looks like this, I know it's best just to leave him alone. What I don't know is what brought this on.

Whatever it is, I guess Trent takes the hint, because a few minutes later, he steps outside by himself, looking less than thrilled. Brenda doesn't notice, and that's just as well. But Jamie catches me looking in his direction and I know he's aware I've seen the tense exchange. The next thing I know he's at my side.

"What time does the gym close?" he asks.

It's his not-so-subtle way of saying that he thinks I should leave.

He's right. I've made as good a first impression as I can manage with Brenda. Better to leave looking relatively cool rather than show myself for the geek I truly am.

"Say hi to Mom," Jamie says.

I nod.

The guy from the big club with the red vest and the bullet eyes gives me a hard look as I move toward the door, and even with warm and fuzzy thoughts of Brenda in my head, I can't help feeling a shiver of fear.

Chapter
4

It's a twenty-minute drive from Trollop's barn to my gym, which is housed in a now-shuttered department store on the main street of St. Thomas. I love summer evenings like this, when it feels like it will stay light forever.

I'm greeted by a familiar voice at the gym door.

"Which way to the beach?"

It's Jake Doyle, my workout buddy from the football team. He's striking a bodybuilder pose and, as he pumps a bicep, he points dramatically off to one side and says, "The beach is that way."

Jake's my best friend on the team. He's also my best friend, period. My "brother from another mother." That said, there's no way I'd ever take him to a biker barbecue or party. He's got an innocence about him, almost like he's younger than he really is, and that crowd would freak him out. Worse, he might really love it.

I've seen Jake's Muscle Beach routine hundreds of times, and I'm not surprised to see it again today. It's still kind of funny, though. In a way, he's making fun of himself. Jake's not the biggest, strongest guy you'll ever see, especially on a football team like ours, which is pretty solid and usually in contention for the city championship. He's also not as scrawny as he was back in grade nine, when he started the joke. But he's definitely not Muscle Beach material either.

He gives me a long look, like he's wondering what's on my mind.

"Things good?" he asks.

"For sure," I mumble, shutting down the conversation. That's as close as we generally come to sharing feelings.

I'm not about to spew about Brenda, or about anything that went on at the barbecue—not the Popeyes appearance or Jamie and Trent. It would all be too hard to explain, and what can Jake do about it anyway? Better just to do what we can do, which right now is pushing weights.

Jake's not one to pry. That's one of the reasons we're friends.

He makes his pecs dance as we get ready in the locker room.

"Greetings from the Doyle twins," he says. This is one of his standard routines, and it always makes me smile. He seems to be trying extra hard today. Other times, he flexes both of his biceps and says,

"Welcome to the gun show. Please stand back for your own personal safety." There's also his gorilla walk and his security guard walk, when he puffs out his chest and throws his shoulders back, like he's ready to haul rowdy skateboarders out of a mall or kick down a barn door.

Today, the angry rants of some old-school rapper blast from a boom box as we walk onto the gym floor. It's not my favorite workout music, but it'll do. The best is Kendrick Lamar's "King Kunta," which has a funny, straightforward, rebellious vibe I could listen to all day. You won't hear any Lady Gaga or Adele in here. You're more likely to hear vintage hip-hop, like The Notorious B.I.G. Our gym isn't part of some glitzy chain, and we like to think it's a hard-core sweat factory. A few of the other kids from the team work out here, but not too many. The more well-off players like the local branch of a club that's advertised on TV, or else they have nice workout areas in their homes.

That's fine with me. I like that this place isn't jam-packed all the time. It's kind of like our little secret. I get a home-away-from-home feeling that I love when-ever I come here. Over the past few months, as I've rehabilitated my injury, I even missed its nose-peeling stink and the corny-but-true slogans on the walls: "Pain is temporary/pride is forever"; "Do today what others won't, so you can do tomorrow what others can't." For the deep thinkers, there's also, "Granted that I must die, how must I live?" That one kind of takes the air out of me. There are also a couple aimed directly at us football players, like "52 brothers are hard to beat."

I've been back in the gym for about a month. I'm not a hundred percent yet, but I'm starting to feel more like an athlete and less like a therapy case.

Jake and I are like a team within a team. He's a surefire bet to get back onto the squad, even though he's a bit small for the offensive line and too slow to be a starting running back or linebacker.

We open up with some bench presses. We start with twelve repetitions each as a warm-up. The last two have a sharp burn. Next come ten with a higher weight; I'm definitely feeling the final couple of presses. Then it's eight with a slightly higher weight. There's genuine pain now. Finally, we each do six repetitions at our maximum weight. For my final two, Jake's guiding the bar with two fingers on each hand. I trust him, which allows me to go as hard as I'm capable of.

"Nasty exertion," Jake says when I'm done. "Forgot my air spray. Forgot you were coming."

"Didn't stink until you walked in," I reply.

"Perhaps you should go a bit easy on the beans," Jake counters. "No judgment. Just a suggestion. Actually a plea. On behalf of humanity and all other living things."

I've got a pretty fair sweat going, even though the front door's propped open to allow some wind in.

"This is the year of the J-Man," Jake says.

Since grade nine, Jake and I have sweated and even bled a little together in practices and games, cried in defeat, and held our helmets high in triumph. We're both graduating next June, and Jake knows this is the last season he straps on a helmet. He wants it to be a big one. If all goes well for him, he might finally be a starter at center.

"Time to get aboard the J-Train," Jake continues. "Next stop, city championship! Best years of our lives, bro."

He might even believe that last line, although I can see Jake being happy with a nice little family in a couple of years. They'll all be good years for Jake, just in different ways. And he knows I hate it when people say that your high-school years are the best ones of your life. Is the rest of life really that bad?

"Pretty soon, you'll be getting paid to do this stuff," Jake says. "Don't forget us little people."

I've had coaches say I've got a legitimate shot at the pros. I also know I'm just one hit in the knee away from pumping gas or serving coffee at a drive-through forever. I breathe in hard and exhale harder, doing seated shoulder presses.

"This is it, brother!" Jake chirps. "Make it good. It's all downhill after this."

I don't know whether to laugh or swear at him, so I zone him out and push through the pain instead.

"Make those university scouts love you," Jake says. "No woman ever will."

No one in my family's ever gone to university, but my coach thinks that I can and should. It's kind of a rush, and I'm flattered when he talks about how I could handle the next level both in schoolwork and in football. He was a pretty good university player himself and had a few pro tryouts, so he knows what he's talking about.

"Put our little borough on the map," Jake says.

I don't hate our town. There are times I feel really comfortable here, but plenty of other times I feel like I'm rotting. I also can't shake the feeling that if I don't get out soon, I'll never leave.

"Got some catching up to do," I say.

"Record it for posterity," Jake says, gesturing toward the book in my hand. "Someday the Hall of Fame will be begging for these notebooks."

We record all of our lifts on paper so we can't kid ourselves about whether or not we're making progress. You are either getting better or falling behind. There are no ties. Someone has to win. Why not us?

I see a friend of Jamie's from years ago on the other side of the gym. His name is Dave Hanson; he's now a cop. I've seen him around a lot less since he got his uniform and Jamie started wearing his Annihilators patch and stopped stammering so much.

I haven't seen Dave here in a while. He's focused pretty intensely on his workout, so we don't have to interrupt the flow of things with some awkward "Hi, how are you, how have you been?" session. It's been almost ten years since he and Jamie were friends, I realize.

Back in the locker room, Jake strikes another pose before a mirror. He knows it embarrasses me, which is half the fun for him.

"You may be a beast but I'm the beauty," he says, grinning at his own joke.

"No one drafted us into this army," he continues. Jake's been saying things like that to pump himself up since he had a squeaky little voice back in grade nine. In those days, most of the girls in our class were taller than us. Several also had deeper voices.

Back then, everything was scary. Football didn't strike me as any more dangerous than riding the bus with a bunch of strange big kids. If I was going to get beaten up, it might as well be by athletes, who I considered a better class of bullies.

Some of the veterans on the team were twice as big as us; once, when we clearly didn't know what we were doing, one of them picked us both up and carried us under his arms like pylons to the right spot on the field. I remember telling Jamie that night that I was going to quit.

"We all get scared," Jamie said. "If you wait to not be scared, it's not going to happen. Besides, what about Jake? You going to leave the little runt out there all by himself?"

Jamie was right, and I've always remembered that pep talk. Ultimately, it was giddy stuff to feel like part of a pack, even if we were experiencing it from a prime viewing spot on the bench. We still wore the purple and gold and we still felt invincible.

Our coach uses the phrase "earned confidence" a lot. It's drilled into us that if we work hard and smart then we've earned the right to be confident. We are also conditioned to visualize success, to stay positive, and to keep thinking of the next right thing to do. The idea is to work our way into the Zone, a magical place where there is no room for panic. In the Zone, we just read the situation, process it, and attack. We don't doubt.

"How's the leg feel?" Jake asks.

"Minty fresh. Thanks for asking."

The status of my leg has been a tender topic since the city championship game nine months ago, when I caught a fullback's helmet square on my left thigh. I'd had nine quarterback sacks in six games leading into this one, which is really good in a league where there's not much passing. I even had back-to-back sacks in our semifinal game—a big reason why we won, despite a shaky performance from our offense. That pretty well iced the game for us and got me a couple of star stickers to put on my helmet and a nice little mention in the *Sun-Sentinel*.

Then I got hit by the fullback, my leg swelled up instantly, and there was no way to Zone my way around that. Jake was one of the guys who helped me off the field. We were both crying a little, although we've never spoken of that. My leg hurt so badly I immediately assumed the worst. Was this going to be my last time on a football field? The team would figure out how to go on, but what about me? I wouldn't let anyone take me to the hospital until after the game; I wanted to cheer on Jake and the guys. We won that championship game, but I couldn't help but wonder if it was all over for me.

"What do you call your injury again?" Jake asks.

"Myositis ossificans."

I can actually pronounce it now. It means that your muscle calcifies and literally becomes like stone. It's serious enough, but fixable.

"Still doing physio?"

"Couple times a week. No more heat or electronic stimulation, and I don't need the whirlpool so much. Lots of stretching, and my physio's got me going to yoga."

"*Namaste*, bro," Jake says. He pauses for a beat and then adds, "It's good, though?"

"Doctor gave me full clearance."

Jamie told me a couple of weeks ago that you don't always get a second chance in life, and that I couldn't blow mine. It's not that often that I totally agree with my brother these days, but on that day, I did.

When we get out to the parking lot, Jake pauses, as if he wants to ask again if something's wrong. He looks concerned, even worried. I guess I'm not hiding my anxiousness about everything that happened at the party as well as I think I am. I know he'd love to help, if there was something he could actually do.

Then he shifts back to the Jake I'm used to.

"Love to stay and chat but some cheerleaders want to oil me down," he says. "No need to get jealous; it's not as great as it sounds. More of a responsibility."

He strides away while I roll my eyes.

Chapter

5

On my way home, I swing by the townhouse where Brenda is staying. It's not really even a decision. I just find myself driving there.

The place is owned by an Annihilator named Mark Goldberg. His dad is a successful dentist in Montreal, and Jamie tells me he'd be surprised if Mark is with the club five years down the line. He'll go back to life among the rich folks once his slumming adventure gets old. For now, though, his townhouse is a good place for people connected with the club to crash.

I don't see Carlito's bike parked outside, a good sign for sure. Maybe I misinterpreted those looks between him and Brenda.

The townhouse's garage door is open, which is odd. Biker hangouts aren't known for their open-door policy. Easier to keep secrets when no one can see what you're up to. Looking more closely, I'm startled to see Jamie there in the shadows, talking to someone. The anxious feeling I've been trying to ignore intensifies.

I slow the car to a crawl and roll down the window so I can shout something to my brother.

Then I see Trent.

Even through the shadows, I can see he looks dead serious, even afraid. Jamie has his hands balled up into fists, and Trent is cringing, leaning back. Jamie could destroy him in no time, and his body language says he knows it.

Jamie's so focused that he doesn't even notice me. He's got his scary face on, the one I remember from when he fought back against our father for the first time. He's staring directly at Trent, close enough to him to drop him with a punch. Then he puts his hands on Trent's shoulders so that he can't move. They're almost nose to nose. I know that Jamie sometimes headbutts people in this position. He could break Trent's nose or knock him out in an instant. I lean out the window, trying to hear what's going on.

"Just listen!" Jamie is saying. His voice has that high pitch it takes on when he's really worked up. That's how he sounded the night he drove Dad out of the house for hitting Mom. At that moment, Jamie's eyes reminded me of Dad at his worst. There was something burning and dark deep inside of him, something dreadful to stare into. Most of the time, Jamie's eyes are soft and hazel and gentle, like Mom's. Not that night. Not tonight either.

Jamie definitely wouldn't want me barging in now. I slowly pull away, hoping they don't see me.

—◄o►—

Mom has already gone to work at the dollar store by the time I get home. After her late shifts, she sometimes gets a ride home from a friend, and often those friends are guys, but I try not to overthink things. She gets home when she gets home.

The rowhouse where we live is no mansion, but I've got the attic pretty much to myself. I plan to move out at the end of the school year. That's when, if all goes well, I'll be getting ready for my first university training camp.

I'm greeted at the door by our dog, a lap-sized Cairn terrier named Eddie who struts around like he's a full-grown rottweiler. What he lacks in size he more than makes up for in attitude.

Eddie's somehow always at the window wagging his tail when I pull up in the Cruze. He doesn't jump around and wildly run up and down the stairs like he used to during his puppy days, but he still makes a pretty good fuss. I know Mom is surprised by how much she loves him but she does. Part of it, I think, is just the feeling of having another loving heart beating under our roof. I'll miss Eddie when I finally move out.

I slip off my shoes at the front door and wait. Eddie sneaks behind me and takes one of them in his mouth. Then he darts past me and deposits the shoe in the living room. It's our little ritual: he loves it when I chase him as he races by. Then Eddie heads back for the other shoe and tries to bait me into chasing him again. If I shout at him, it's even better. I know he won't really hide or ruin my shoes, and he knows I'm not really trying to catch him. We all like our games, I guess.

I go to the fridge for a bottle of water before I head toward the attic and my bed. That takes me past the spot in the kitchen that always makes me flinch—the corner next to the dishwasher where Jamie dropped Dad with a crisp left to the chin that night, a decade ago. I'm not sure who was more surprised, my brother or my father. The expression on Dad's face as he looked up from the linoleum was one of absolute shock. He stared at Mom as if he expected some sort of support, and then realized it was all over.

Dad's long gone now and I guess that's best for all of us. He married a woman with a couple of kids of her own that he met in his new apartment building and we haven't seen him much over the past few years. He now lives in Byron, on the edge of London, which means we could see each other if either of us wanted to make a little drive, but we don't.

Dad deserved that shot in the mouth that day, but he wasn't always so bad. In fact, I can remember a time when he was my hero. When I was really young and afraid of shadows and the dark, Dad would look under my bed to check for monsters and then smile and reassure me that everything was going to be okay. I believed him. That feels like so long ago.

Dad's a bricklayer and he did some work as a stonemason too. All that manual labor took its toll on his back and knees, so he never played sports or even spent much time outside with me when he got off work. He just tried to relax, and often relaxing meant drinking.

It has been a long day. It's late and I need rest. I know better than to wait up for Mom. She won't get off work for a couple more hours, and by the time she gets home, I'll be sound asleep.

It's a little before midnight when my head hits the pillow. But when I'm finally lying in bed, I can't sleep. It hits me just how uneasy I feel about what I saw in the townhouse garage between Jamie and Trent, and I think again about all the strange vibes at the barn earlier today. There's always drama with bikers. Drama's part of the reason they're in the club, I think. Sometimes they have to do stupid things to make their lives seem interesting and to get attention, and it can be hard to tell how seriously to take the theatrics. Then there are the Popeyes. There's something cold about them, even icy. They just hung around in the background at Trollop's party, taking it all in. They didn't seem to want attention at all, and this scares me even more.

Chapter 6

I sleep in the morning after the party, in preparation for the night shift I've pulled at work. When I get out of bed, my body's a bit tight from the workout, which is a good feeling in a way. I'm wondering what Brenda and Jamie have been up to since I last saw them, but I try not to dwell on troubling thoughts.

Mom's in the kitchen when I stumble in around nine.

"Can I make you an omelet?" she asks. "Scrambled eggs? My boy needs his protein."

"Wow. Western omelet would be great."

"Coming right up."

She's extra cheerful this morning. It's sweet she's in her homemaker mode, but I suspect she'll serve up some questions along with my breakfast.

"You saw Jamie yesterday?"

Here we go.

"Yup. At Trollop's."

She doesn't like Trollop, but over the years she has learned to tolerate him.

"He look okay?"

She's talking about Jamie, not Trollop. Trollop never looks okay.

How do I answer that? That last time I saw Jamie, he definitely didn't look okay, and at the moment, I'm just hoping he didn't pound the crap out of Brenda's big brother. But I can't say any of that.

"Yeah, seemed okay, but I didn't talk with him much."

Mom gets the code here. I don't want her mining me for information about Jamie. I avoid eye contact as I turn on the coffeemaker.

"Maybe I'll give him a call," Mom says.

"Sure," is the best I can do as I attack a protein shake along with the omelet.

I appreciate that Mom's trying, and I hate to see her worry about Jamie—but I'm worried too. Things seem more tense in Jamie's world now that the Popeyes are hanging around.

To be fair, Jamie has worried about us too. Things were pretty awful right after Dad left. Mom started to crumble. There was crying and anger and, sometimes, I got the feeling Mom resented Jamie for driving Dad away. Other times, she seemed to treat him like a hero. In those days, Mom had no trouble attracting boyfriends. She just couldn't keep them. There were construction workers and a teacher and a couple of guys who I think were in sales. Once or twice, I came close to having a half brother or sister courtesy of a new blended family, but those situations always fell through. Jamie showed up at the house in his Annihilators colors on occasion, when he wanted to send one boyfriend or another on his way. He didn't threaten them; he didn't have to. He just didn't smile much and they got the message.

I remember one of Mom's boyfriends walking into the living room when I was about eleven. I was watching one of those corny TV sitcoms where a wise father gives valuable life advice to his kids. "That's not real life," the boyfriend said. "Real people don't talk like that." I was happy when he moved on.

Once I got to know Jake Doyle's family, I realized that guy was wrong. There *are* families that talk like that! Jake's family lives in a tidy subdivision where the appliances are new and functional. At Jake's place, they don't panic when something doesn't work. They just fix it themselves, call in someone to repair it, or get a new one. I should head over to their place sometime soon for a shot of normalness. The Doyles have told me I'm always welcome, and they actually mean it.

"What's up for you today?" I ask Mom.

"I have to wait around for the Internet guy. Why can't they just give you a time when they'll come by?"

Mom tends to look at everything that goes wrong in our lives as a personal insult or failure or attack, but that's not the way it is at Jake's place. Jake's mom doesn't blame God or the universe or karma or the government or herself or someone else when things don't work. She just takes care of it and keeps on smiling.

There was a time, back in grade nine, when Jake and I were at his place for a sleepover and he decided to empty the dishwasher, without being asked. I helped out and it only took five minutes or so.

You would have thought he'd given his mother a new fully loaded Volvo.

"You're such a good son," she said, and hugged him.

Then she gave me a little hug too. That actually took my breath away.

◄o►

After breakfast, it's off to the park for some stretches and running drills. I love how I can lose myself in football and all the training that goes with it. I started working out with our school's track team a couple of years ago, and while I'm no sprinter I found that working alongside real runners helped my acceleration on the field. I lift my knees higher and swing my arms more efficiently now. Hurdling has also taught me to stretch my hips, which really helps.

Today, I run a series of seven sprints with a twenty-second rest in between. The sprints range from twenty to forty yards, simulating a drive in a game.

By the time training camp opens, I'll have it down to fourteen-second rests between sets, and I'll increase the number of sets to nine.

I don't go flat out today because I'm still testing my leg. Once I'm done, I'm a bit gassed but the leg feels fine. I switch to a series of drills running around cones. That forces me to change direction at speed and get low, a bit like during a game.

There was a time when I would get self-conscious working out alone in the park. Now I don't even think of anyone else.

Mom's out when I return home for a little nap but I'm okay with that. It's not like we constantly check in with each other. Eddie's full of pep as usual and makes his presence known, scooting off with my shoes again. It's hard to feel alone with him around. My nap turns into a fitful six-hour sleep. I dream of something that leaves me with an unsettled feeling when I finally awake.

I switch on the TV news. There's nothing too shocking locally, so I guess Jamie couldn't have done anything too horrible with Trent. This eases my mind, if only a little. Then I switch over to cable sports and allow my thoughts to drift back to Brenda. I wonder what she's been doing all day, if she has plans tonight, if she's thought about me at all. It's a much better way to kill time than worrying about Jamie.

But I can't get rid of those thoughts completely. Around nine in the evening, I start getting ready for work. My shift doesn't start until eleven, but I like getting places early. As I'm figuring out what to wear—it comes down to a choice of what's clean and not too wrinkled—I think again about the scene outside the townhouse. The anger in Jamie's face and the look of fear on Trent's. My mind also drifts to Carlito and Brenda, and I wonder again what the history there is. Carlito has a baby face that girls find cute but is totally at odds with how I see him. There's an unwanted image in my head of Carlito leaning over Brenda in an intimate way and it makes me sick and angry. Another image: her feeling safe with his tough-guy act. Wanting him. Smiling. Submitting. Encouraging. That makes me feel even worse.

Chapter 7

I work overnight shifts at our local newspaper, the *Sun-Sentinel*. I got the job a couple of weeks ago through the defensive-line coach, who's also my old English teacher. He used to play college ball with one of the editors there and he put in a good word for me. It's the first time anyone in my family has worked at what could be considered a white-collar job.

I'm a radio room night stalker, and I work from 11:00 p.m. to 7:00 a.m., three nights a week. I monitor ambulance and fire department scanners and various police and community Twitter feeds and anything else of local interest I find on the Internet. I also copy links to trending stories in other media and send them around to our reporters and editors. The pay is okay, the job is often interesting, and I'm left with plenty of time for the gym.

Part of my job is fielding random calls from the public and summarizing their complaints and suggestions for the editors. Often, I make notes about possible leads for the daytime reporters. It's a good feeling when they take my tips seriously and follow up on them, and I see the resulting stories in the paper and on the webpage.

It's solitary work and that suits me. Sometimes I think the newsroom's like a lighthouse—a silent sentinel watching over the whole world, overseeing everything and taking note of only the most interesting, meaningful things—though I definitely don't talk like that when I'm there, and neither does anyone else. Thoughts like that feel like delicate little bubbles; beautiful but easily destroyed.

In the newsroom tonight, it's just me, an older police reporter named Bill Taylor, and the cleaner, a Portuguese woman who is just starting her shift.

Bill took a buyout from the *Toronto Star* a few years ago after working there for decades. His cop daughter who lives in London had recently given birth to a daughter with Down syndrome and he wanted to be closer to them. He's not snotty about working here, even though he has worked in far better places.

There's a big electronic board in the newsroom that tracks the number of "clicks" for each story on the paper's webpage. The top items on today's board include "Passenger turns violent after being told he can't do yoga on plane," a video of a trio of waterskiing albino squirrels from somewhere in Europe, and another of a monkey riding a pig like a horse, but backward. The most popular video this week is a semi-tasteful item about a group of women roller-skating topless past a local construction site to make some political point about nipples. Close behind it is a bikinied Swedish cop tackling some lout during an off-duty arrest on a beach. Further down the popularity board are stories on the high costs of housing for seniors, delays in cancer treatment, and the election of a new school board chairperson.

"You're working late," I say to Bill, pointing out the obvious.

"Late-breaking nipple-skating update," he replies. Then he mutters, "Responsible sensationalism."

Another pause, and then Bill adds: "We do what we have to do so we can do what we want to do."

Bill reminds me of Ripper somehow. Maybe it's that they both seem to know when to keep calm and accept things and when to fight back.

Bill's desk is organized chaos. I'm sure he has a pretty good idea which papers and files are piled where, and he doesn't seem to care what the rest of us think. Over Bill's desk is a sign that reads, *Illegitimi non carborundum*, which I'm told translates roughly to "Don't let the bastards grind you down." Under that is a saying attributed to English poet John Milton: "Let her [Truth] and Falsehood grapple; who ever knew Truth put to the worse in a free and open encounter?"

"Can I ask you a question?" I ask.

"You just did. Want to ask another one? Sure." Bill loves his corny jokes. Someone has to. Come to think of it, he and Jake would get along great.

"Heard anything about what's going on with the Annihilators?"

I'm a bit anxious that I haven't heard from Jamie since the party. And Bill is surprisingly knowledgeable about cops and bikers, although I'm not quite sure why. He's also cool about sharing his information and expertise with me.

"Yeah. Tense times. Popeyes are moving in. This could be the summer they set up a clubhouse of their own here."

"Yeah. Just seems tenser. Different."

It certainly had looked like something was about to snap between Jamie and Trent at the party, and at Goldberg's townhouse. No matter how hard I try, I can't push it to the back of my mind. And Trollop was obviously trying to impress the new bikers who were at the party, but why? I can't shake the feeling that something horrible is about to happen; maybe it already has. It didn't just feel like the usual rude fun at Trollop's party. It felt like a powder keg about to explode.

Bill holds my gaze a little longer than he needs to. He must know who Jamie is, although we've never discussed it. Our town is a small enough place.

"How would the Popeyes coming to town affect the Annihilators?" I ask.

"The big club could quietly swallow them up. Biker

version of a hostile takeover. Or a python eating a pig. Or a rat."

Again the word "rat." An image of Trollop's T-shirt pops into my head; I force it out and listen to what Bill is saying. "Crystal meth is cheap and pays big. You don't have the bother of sneaking it past borders. You just cook it up yourself. Some of the Annihilators have been dealing in meth, just on a small-time basis so far, but that could change. I wouldn't be surprised if the Popeyes try to step in and take it all over."

"What's the big deal about St. Thomas?" I ask.

Bill stuffs a couple of folders from his desk into his briefcase, pushes his chair away from his computer, and slips his glasses into his shirt pocket. Enough writing for today.

"Nothing really. Except that it's close to London, and London's a good market. It's on the highway. It's got a university and a college, which means lots of potential customers. The Popeyes like universities and colleges and highways. It's also small enough that they can get cozy with the local cops."

"But why would the Annihilators just let them move in? And invite them to parties?"

"Not all of the local club members want the Popeyes here. It's dicey. It's basically Trollop's group that's pushing for it."

"Why now?"

"That skinny guy that the Annihilators have found is a good cook. The Julia Child of the meth world."

He's obviously talking about Trent. He grins like he has just told a real knee-slapper, but I don't have a clue who Julia Child is.

Bill continues: "The Popeyes will want a big piece of the local action or else they'll try to shut it down. They're not going to back away from some Mickey Mouse regional club."

He watches my face as he says "Mickey Mouse." Then he continues: "And if they don't scoop up the Annihilators and absorb them, their rivals will."

He gestures for me to sit down in a chair near his.

"Who would you call the Popeyes' rivals?"

"There's the Outlaws. They're international too."

"There's not much of an Outlaw presence around here though, is there?"

"No, but they might come in if they pick up the scent of money. They might want to pull in the skinny cook too."

"What if the rest of the Annihilators say no to joining the Popeyes?"

Bill makes a little pistol shape with his fingers. "They don't like the word no. Also, they've got to worry about the Spartans, the other club around here, right? Some of the Spartans would love to join the Popeyes. Other Spartans would love to join up with some of the Annihilators to hold off the Popeyes."

It's a bit dizzying, like history class when we learned about how hostilities in the Balkans somehow led to the start of World War I. The Annihilators and the Spartans, both from London, are the two biker clubs in our area. For the most part, the Spartans seem to know their place in the biker world. I haven't heard of them starting stupid beefs by acting tough in out-of-town bars, and they've had no rats that I've heard of. They've had some pretty tough members in the past, including one guy who'd supposedly tattooed the name of every police officer who ever arrested him onto his arms, to remind him to get them back someday. The Spartans have had a few conflicts with the Annihilators over the years, especially during a period some years ago when Trollop was in power. Generally, though, the Spartans and the Annihilators stay out of each other's hair.

"Whatever shakes out, I don't see Trollop fitting in to the big club," Bill continues. "No matter how much he sucks up to them."

"Why?"

He pauses for a second and then says, "He's got a knack for attracting problems. Trollop's serving a life sentence to his own stupidity."

He's obviously pretty pleased with that line. From what I've seen, though, it's accurate. Bill knows things, although I'm not sure where he's getting his information. It can't all be from cops.

A few minutes later, Bill's gone for the day and I'm alone in the radio room. There's the usual run of telephone calls.

"Can you tell me what's happened to Gary Carson?" a lonely sounding senior asks.

He's talking about a humor columnist who was popular back when I was in about grade seven and who died two or three years ago. I don't have the heart to relay this.

"I think he's taking a break," I say instead.

"Must be nice," the senior says.

I'm also monitoring whether a local teenage stabbing victim is getting better or worse, which involves calls every forty-five minutes or so to the police. It could go either way in the next few hours, as I understand it. I can't imagine what his family is going through, and I try not to.

The phone rings again.

"My apartment, it's full of cockroaches," a man who sounds middle-aged says. "I keep spraying it and they're still here."

The man's anger builds as he tells me that he's coughing up blood and the insecticide isn't working.

"Can you open a window?" I suggest.

He dismisses that like it's crazy talk and hangs up on me.

I wonder if these callers have any clue that I'm seventeen. Maybe it doesn't matter. They just need someone to talk to out there in the dark.

The calls slow down and my mind drifts back to Brenda at the party yesterday afternoon. Was she really as amazing as I remember her? Could anyone be? Around midnight, I find her on Facebook. I had looked her up before, when she was still at our school, but never had the guts to make a friend request.

She's online too, and before I know it I have a new Facebook friend.

I'm at work and a little stir-crazy, I type.

Where's work?

The paper. I just monitor the Internet for breaking news and other stuff.

It's kind of a cool job, and I'm happy to have a chance to impress her. I'm trying to act casual but I'm pretty proud of the job myself. It's the first work I've done that hasn't involved wearing a name tag; in the past I've been a fast-food slinger and a dishwasher and I worked in the laundry room of an old folks' home, which was particularly nasty.

Wow.

I love that she typed that.

What's up with you?

Not so much.

That's good news already. If Jamie had leveled Trent, I'd hear about it now.

Time to relax. I'm still queasy about the Popeyes, but a weight lifts from my mind nonetheless.

It's hard to imagine someone as beautiful as Brenda being alone and bored at night, but here she is, chatting with me. I picture a parade of athletes and actors and rock stars and business moguls lined up outside her door, nervously holding bouquets of flowers as they vie for her smile. I try not to put bikers like Carlito in the picture too.

I take a deep breath as I decide to up my game.

Wish we were having this chat on a desert island, I type. I cringe right after I hit Send.

Anyone else on that island?

I hold my breath and go on.

No one close.

Good.

I don't push it further but my heart is racing. Is she toying with me?

Big smile, I type.

She sends back a happy face emoticon.

Tonight the moon looks like a big happy bubble. I wonder how many other people are looking up at it. Maybe she's one of them.

A couple of seconds later, another message beeps through. *I should let you get back to work.* It feels like a rejection until she adds, *Talk soon?*

Sounds great. Soon.

And with that, she's gone.

Chapter 8

I like to have breakfast at a little diner nearby after pulling a night shift. It helps me wind down, if I go easy on the coffee. Today, a gentle rain starts up as I drive past a Walmart, a McDonald's, and lots of tired looking mom-and-pop businesses. The diner's just a few minutes off the main highway, beside a tattoo parlor. I can't deny that my hometown is a bit of a backwater, but I still feel comfortable here, at least most of the time.

I replay my Facebook conversation with Brenda in my mind as I drive. She didn't throw herself at me, but her tone definitely held some promise. Even that promise is enough to send my stomach into backflip mode. I can't remember ever feeling like this about a girl before. And it isn't just her looks, either. More like her aura. Some sort of spark. Much more than that, really. A force field. It's like I already know her, instead of just imagining that I do. Just looking at us, you'd wonder why a girl like her would be interested in getting to know a guy like me, but she seems happy enough to be doing it, which is all that counts. Maybe she's just very good at being polite, or maybe I analyze things too much and should just enjoy the moment.

Even if things do click between the two of us, I won't be bringing her home to meet Mom anytime soon. Mom does her best, most of the time, but I'm still not so comfortable with friends, even old friends, dropping by my place, let alone someone like Brenda. Jake's house isn't always spotless or super tidy, but it's never embarrassing. At my house, there's a good chance the place will be a mess. There's also a chance that, no matter the time of day, Mom will have had a drink or two, and I don't need kids at school hearing about that. Mom likes to act as if she's had some big, interesting past, but that never really happened, and it's awful to see her in a conversation when her face turns sad and lost. And I *definitely* don't need a girl I like having to make small talk with one of Mom's boyfriends. I wonder what Brenda's home life is like.

I turn left a little ways past the larger-than-life-sized elephant statue at the side of the road. Here, more than a hundred years ago, poor Jumbo—the giant star of the Barnum & Bailey Circus—was killed by a locomotive after he broke free from the local fairgrounds. I've never heard of another circus coming to town, but there's been a Jumbo statue here for as long as I can remember. We do seem to like our losers. I prefer to think of Jumbo in heroic terms: that he died making a stand, charging headlong down the tracks, nostrils flaring and tusks lowered, defiant and uncompromising and fully alive. In that instant, it didn't matter that his plight was utterly hopeless.

Aside from Jumbo, St. Thomas is best known as the home of a star NHL defenseman, as a former manufacturing hub for faucets, and as a stop, years ago, on the Underground Railroad. That last part, at least, is pretty cool.

The diner's just a few blocks past the bronze elephant. It's clean and homey and famous for its cheeseburgers (named "Jumbos," of course), a greasy comfort food you can order any time of the day: I don't know why anyone would want a cheeseburger at 9:00 a.m., but apparently some folks do. Lack of a full night's sleep has me feeling a bit dreamy, and I trick myself into imagining Brenda waiting for me at a table as I walk in. (You probably won't be surprised to hear that I'm not so experienced with girls. I'm technically a virgin, unless you count . . . Nope, no need to go there. You're still a virgin if no one else is involved.)

I quickly order a Western omelet. It's what I normally get—plenty of protein and pretty much impossible to screw up.

The table next to me is empty when I place my order, but a couple of minutes later, two chubby preschool-aged girls arrive with a woman in her fifties or sixties. It would be easy for a cartoonist to make the girls look like little piggies: nature has helped by giving them round cheeks and upturned snout-like noses. I'm guessing the woman with them is their grandmother. She's wearing a black sweatshirt decorated on the back with sequined silver wolves baying at the moon, and it's unzipped to reveal a T-shirt bearing the message "Grandchildren are God's reward for not killing your children."

I've seen her somewhere before, although I can't quite place it.

A couple of minutes after they sit down, the bigger of the two girls makes a grab for the can of soda across the table. The granny blocks her hand and gives her an earnest, tough-love scowl.

"No more Coke 'till you finish your cheeseburger," she admonishes.

She shifts her weight so she can face me directly. "They're my daughter's kids," she explains. "They won't eat vegetables and I've got to feed them something."

It's morning, and you'd think they'd be eating porridge or pancakes or something like that, but I'm too tired to ask. Thanks to my night shift, I've had enough of weird humanity.

Granny gives me a hard look.

"I know you from somewhere," she says. "You a friend of Carlito's?"

"We've met," I say. Figures, I think.

She turns back to the kids and I scarf the rest of

my omelet. It's time to settle the bill and get out. She's either a family friend of Carlito's or actual family. Either way, I don't feel like chatting. I wonder if the woman has ever met Brenda.

The hard-eyed Nomad that I saw at the barn party yesterday is coming through the diner door as I walk out. He's wearing a regular black leather jacket now, not the red Kevlar vest he had on then. With his rigid walk and stern expression, you'd think he's a police sergeant or something, despite the outlaw chic. He gives me what could be a tight-faced nod, although it might just be a twitch. He doesn't actually stop, so he can't really want to talk. I'd hate to be alone in a confined space with him; he looks like a guy who's fully prepared to inflict some serious damage on anyone who gets in his way. My little town is getting crowded.

◄o►

The Annihilators' clubhouse is just a few minutes down the road from the diner, and some people in town like to joke that if its walls could talk, they'd be in a witness protection program. It's a shack with dirty siding and a hillbilly-style front balcony on a street that looks like an alley, with no sidewalks and not enough room for two cars to pass each other in opposite directions.

I've heard that clubhouses in Toronto and Montreal are built like bunkers, but the Annihilators' place certainly doesn't fit into that category. Trollop and his little circle of idiots have hung security cameras by the doors and installed bars over the windows, but I can't see them ever doing much good. Since there's almost no front lawn and no fence, it would be ridiculously easy to attack the clubhouse from the street, if anyone cared to. So far, no one has bothered to try.

It seems to me that the Annihilators are the biker equivalent of beer league athletes. That said, there's usually a pretty nice collection of motorcycles parked outside: Harley-Davidsons, Victorys, and Indians. With some of the guys, I get the feeling that their bike is the best thing they'll ever own. Club rules say the bikes have to be North American made, and that members have to clock a certain number of miles between May and the Labor Day weekend, a period they grandly call the Riding Season. It might not sound like much, but it's something they're proud of. In that way, at least, the Annihilators are old-school in a good way. A lot of motorcycle clubs aren't even about the bikes anymore, but our local crew is a bike club that sometimes ventures into crime, rather than a group of felons that occasionally rides motorcycles. For members like Jamie and Ripper, that's an important distinction, although I'm sure plenty of bikers couldn't care less.

There's nothing going on there today that I can see and so I keep on driving. Before I know it, I'm heading past Goldberg's townhouse again. I'm hoping to bump into Brenda so we can have an excuse to talk. As I round the corner I see at least a half dozen police cars. That can't be good. Then I see an ambulance and a mobile police command post. The paramedics don't appear to be in any hurry.

Blood rushes to my face and I can feel my heart pounding against my rib cage. I think again about the tension between Jamie and Trent and then just hope I'm worrying about nothing.

Brenda's standing near the roadway. There are those eyes again, those soft bunny rabbit eyes, but this time, she's pale and trembling and scared. She looks like she's in shock. I can see she's been crying. A lot.

All the action's centered on the garage.

A Volvo SUV with a sign reading "CORONER, Dr. Edward James" in the back window pulls up by the police command post. A man of about sixty with a shock of graying hair steps out. His glasses are perched at the end of his nose and his hair is trimmed in a brush cut, only higher.

"Dr. James," one of the cops says and leads him toward the garage.

He's calm enough. I imagine he has been to plenty of nasty crime and accident scenes. It's time to go, before the attention shifts from him to me.

As I press on the gas pedal, another police car pulls up and Brenda gets in the back. For an instant, she's alongside me. I've thought of her almost nonstop since the party, but I've never once imagined the lost expression I see on her face.

Her eyes meet mine and she mouths some words. I can make them out clearly even though I can't hear her. They couldn't hit me harder if she was screaming them out loud.

"He's dead."

Chapter
9

The police cruiser pulls away and there's no chance to ask Brenda who's dead.

I never got out of my car as I drove past the townhouse, so I must have looked like just another rubbernecker. Now I drive away slowly, trying not to attract attention.

I sweat a lot when I get panicky, and my shirt's sticking to my back now. I take deep breaths to try to maintain control. I feel like I'm a little kid, lost and being chased and unable to defend myself, even though in reality I'm bigger and stronger than the average grown man. When I was younger, I was constantly on the edge of panic attacks when Mom and Dad fought. I always feared the moment when things would go really crazy and life as I knew it would end in some awful explosion of violence. It doesn't help that I haven't slept since my night shift and I feel a little tipsy.

I drive slowly, so that no one notices me.

When Brenda said, "He's dead," did she mean Jamie? A rush of dread washes over me. I can't even imagine Mom's face if someone had to give her that news. I can't imagine my own.

Or did she mean Trent?

On the drive home, I play out the various scenarios in my mind, trying to decide which one is most likely. No matter how I spin it, either Jamie or Trent is lying dead at the end. As I pull up to our place, I pray I don't bump into Mom. She'll sense that something is wrong as soon as she sees me or hears my voice, and I don't need a scene. I need to calm down and figure things out, not add drama.

Eddie runs down the stairs to greet me as I walk into the house.

"Mom?"

No answer.

"Mom?"

Still nothing.

Now Eddie is jumping around my feet. I suppose he's hoping I'll take off my shoes so he can run away with them. Why can't humans be this easy to understand and satisfy?

I don't see Mom's jacket or shoes by the front door. It's a small blessing, I suppose, that she's out, although it would be nice to know where she is.

If Trent's dead, is Jamie in trouble? There was

obviously something going on between them at the party and the townhouse. If it's Jamie . . .

I can't even think about that.

My heart is thumping. My shirt is still stuck to my back. I need to keep my breathing under control. I have to face the possibility that my brother might be dead. Our family isn't much as it is. If we lose him . . .

I've lost Jamie before. There was a time, back when I was in grade five, when it seemed like Jamie dropped off the face of the earth. He didn't come by the house for months and months. He'd been working in St. Thomas as a drywaller, but all of a sudden he was gone from town for almost the entire spring. That was when Trollop seemed to be running things in the club and Ripper was out of town working on a big construction project in Toronto. Then Jamie came back with a splash and lots of cash. He got me a baseball glove and a new bike and a skateboard, while Mom got a new washer and dryer. He also had a nice girlfriend named Melanie who talked loudly and brought me jellybeans and licorice when she and Jamie came over to the house. That was the year he gave me and Mom the Cruze as a family Christmas present.

I didn't know where the money came from and I've never asked. Besides, Mom was happy just to have him around again. The house was pretty empty when it was just me and her and Eddie.

This little trip down memory lane makes me realize something: we've had our problems, but we're still a family, and I've never had to deal with the death of someone in my immediate family before. I certainly don't want to start now—which makes this one of those "please God" moments you always see in movies or read about in books. The type where the main character realizes they are on the verge of losing something that really matters and prays with everything they have to stop it from happening. Sometimes it works out in the end and sometimes it doesn't. But right now, in real life, I can't stand the suspense. I need to know what I'm dealing with. I need to know who's dead.

For a minute, I think about calling Brenda, and then remember that doesn't make sense. If she's with the police, she won't be able to talk, and I need to know now.

I've called the hospital before for work, following up on accident reports from the police scanners, and I even know the head nurse. Her son is a pretty good junior varsity player who actually looks up to me. I'll call her first and take it from there.

"Hello, Josh Williams here . . ."

"You okay?"

She can tell by my voice that there's something wrong.

"Um, I'm calling about a death on Lakeview . . ."

"Are you at work, Josh? Someone just called from the paper."

"No," I say. I'm surprised how readily my voice cracks when I'm stressed. "I need to know . . . Is there a person who died . . . ?"

"Yes, there was a fatality there. I'm afraid I can't tell you more. I can only tell family."

"But I need to know . . ."

"I can only tell the family of the person who died," she says again. Then she adds, gently, "I can't tell you because you're not related."

I feel a rush of relief.

Then it hits me: if it's not Jamie who's dead . . .

Brenda is out there alone, coping with the death of her only brother.

I feel a little flash of guilt. My good news might be her bad news. And then I think of some bad news of my own.

It would also likely mean that Jamie is a suspect.

"Thanks," I tell the nurse. "I really appreciate it."

Next, I text Brenda. She gave me her number when we chatted on Facebook.

You okay? I ask. I imagine her alone in a room with a couple of cops. Is she crying? Getting angry at the killers? Blaming Trent's biker buddies? Hopefully she treads lightly. She must know a few things about the meth business if she shared a home with Trent. Passing on details to the police could be dangerous.

I'm getting way ahead of myself here. She hasn't even answered my text yet.

I flip the TV on to the local news but there's nothing about any death yet. My next stop is the *Sun-Sentinel*'s webpage, but there's nothing there either.

Finally, it appears on a London news channel. "There has been a death in a known hangout of the Annihilators biker club." The camera pans over the townhouse. There are plenty of police still around, as well as a couple of neighbors, soaking in the drama. "Sources say that the pressures of a potential biker war between different motorcycle clubs may have resulted in this violent scene," the reporter continues. "Spotted in the area recently are members of the Popeyes, a powerful biker gang with chapters in Toronto and Montreal. The Popeyes are alleged to be involved in serious criminal activities, including the drug trade, extortion, and arson. Police haven't yet released the name of the dead man found in the garage here. Sources say he either lived here or was a frequent visitor.

"It's too early to decide if this was a murder or something else—like suicide," he concludes.

I'm surprised to hear the word "suicide" in the report, but it is a live broadcast and also a small station, so I'm guessing there isn't much supervision. Even with my limited experience, I know that reporters don't like to speculate about possibly self-inflicted deaths unless they absolutely have to.

I wander over to the fridge for a bottle of water, peeling my shirt away from my skin as I go. I'm still sweating hard but at least the thumping of my heart has settled down somewhat.

I text Jamie. It would make life so much easier if he would just stay in touch and give me straight answers when I need them.

A few minutes pass. Jamie is slow to get back at the best of times, I tell myself.

Another try.

Still no reply.

I return to the paper's website and click over to the crime section. At last there's some news, under the headline "Police called to Lakeview town-house." The story is just a few paragraphs long. I call the *Sun-Sentinel* and an intern, Brooklyn Fox, picks up on the fourth ring. We know each other, although I wouldn't say we're friends.

"You cover that call on Lakeview?" I ask.

"Yup. On the phone at least. No biggie."

"But homicide . . ."

She cuts me off. "Duty desk told me off the re-cord"—I can tell she loved saying that—"it might just be a suicide."

"Suicide?" A long pause to gather my breath and then, "Who?"

"Some meth cook. Urban renewal death." The term is cop slang for the death of a person who is a burden upon society, but it always makes me cringe. Would people use that term if Jamie were killed? "Police didn't seem to be sweating it. No biggie. Gotta run."

Click.

And that's that.

So it is Trent who's dead. Meth cook or not, I'm bothered by how lightly the police and our local media seem to be treating it. I saw Trent alive just a couple days ago. Arguing with Jamie. Smiling at Brenda.

Another text to Jamie.

Still no reply.

Mom could come home anytime. I have to get out of the house fast: if she sees me she'll know something's wrong and lose it. She'll panic if I tell her about Jamie's argument with Trent, so that's something I'll have to keep to myself for now, maybe forever.

I still haven't slept since my night shift and I could badly use some rest, but I'm too pumped with adrenaline. I need to get the facts and process them.

I'll deal with Mom later.

Chapter 10

I'*m so sorry*, I text Brenda.

It's early evening now and I still haven't gotten to bed. I can get by on three or four hours of sleep, but I won't be working out today.

I'm not sure if she's free to talk or if she's still down at the police station. The last day must have been hellish for her. Her brother dies and she has to go straight to the station to face what I imagine are some pretty tough questions. It's a murder investigation, after all, and Trent was a known associate of a biker gang.

I wonder when exactly she learned that Trent was dead. Was it hours after we finished chatting on Facebook? Minutes?

Thanks, she replies. The police must be finished with her at last.

Where are you now?

My aunt's.

I'm trying to think of which aunt that might be when she continues: *Can you come get me?*

I don't hesitate: *Where?*

She texts me the address. It's not a great part of town, but we don't have that many great parts of town. There are plenty of streets lined with one-story homes built for the factory workers our town used to have, when we had factories. There are also semis and row-houses, like where I live. They're okay places, but none of it's *Better Homes and Gardens* stuff.

From what I've heard, Trent and Brenda's family are spread around southwestern Ontario in various industrial towns. I don't know that much about her home life, except that she seems to bounce from place to place. I guess that's why she didn't have much of a circle of friends when she was at my school.

Brenda runs out quickly when I pull up outside. She's shaking as she gets into the car and her shoulders are curled inward, as if she's bracing herself against something. She looks whipped.

I must look like a mess myself. I haven't showered in a day, but Brenda doesn't seem to notice. This isn't exactly a date.

"I'm really sorry," I say. I still can't think of anything better.

"Thanks."

She's not so talkative now either.

I drive around for a bit but I don't feel like concentrating on traffic. I hit a McDonald's drive-through and we get a couple smoothies. Neither of us feels like sitting in public. The sun is just starting to set. I park by the Thames River where couples go to neck. At least it's quiet.

"You okay?" I ask.

She doesn't answer me, but she does start crying—and keeps going for what feels like forever but is probably only a few minutes.

"I'm sorry," she finally says.

"No, cry if you want to."

I realize how stupid that must sound. Who wants to cry? And why would she do it on command from me?

I don't know how to ask her about Trent. I figure she'll talk about him when she's ready. If it were me, I'd feel angry and ashamed and overwhelmed. I wouldn't want to talk.

"So . . . why did you leave school?" I finally ask, grasping for a neutral topic of conversation.

She takes a deep breath and lowers her eyes. I thought that would be an easy question, but she looks like she is going to start crying again. "It was so stupid. There was a geography assignment. My answer wasn't long but it was to the point. The teacher gave me a funny look when we got the assignments back. He asked me to stay after class. When everyone was gone, he looked at me and smiled and said he knew that I cheated. He barely knew my name but he figured he knew enough to accuse me of something like that. Then he asked if I knew what plagiarism was."

She watches the river out the window for a while before she continues. "I didn't say anything. I was stunned. Of course I knew! But I wrote the assignment myself. It was all my work, I swear. I'm actually pretty smart, believe it or not. But what was I supposed to say? He'd made up his mind. I walked out and never came back." She shakes her head, as if she still can't really believe the whole thing. "How did he know he could get away with treating me like that? Was it partly because I'm a girl? Because of my family? He wouldn't have been like that if my dad was a teacher or a lawyer or a politician. Or even a biker with a patch." She didn't say what her dad does now. I heard he had worked as a short-order cook for a while after losing his job at a sock factory.

"Nobody screws with Ripper's daughter," she adds. "Someone tried once and . . ."

I've heard that story too. Ripper's a nice guy but you don't want to get him mad, especially when it comes to his family. Brenda takes a deep breath and her tone changes. She doesn't sound like she's about to cry anymore. Now she sounds angry.

"Did you see the news?" she says. "How they're saying it's suicide?"

She's staring off into space as if she's sending her words out into some vast unknown. "Unreal," she continues. "Suicide? Suicide? Since when do reporters talk about suicide?"

"Usually only if it's someone famous or really important," I chime in idiotically, then wonder: Did I just insult her brother? She doesn't seem to notice or mind. Her voice has gone flat now after the flash of temper.

"If I tell you something will you promise . . . ?"

I nod, not needing to hear the rest of the question. "Of course."

Clearly, she needs to talk. We never spoke once in the six months at school when I had a huge crush on her. And now, just a couple of days after meeting properly, she seems to want to tell me something big.

She takes a deep breath. Her eyes are already so red. She's not a little girl but she looks like one right now. I notice that her hair smells like strawberries.

"My dad, he killed himself when I was a little girl."

I have the feeling she's in such deep shock that she would have told anyone who'd listen, but I still feel like we have a connection. Her voice quivers midway through the word "killed" and she rushes out the rest of the sentence, then sighs. "I don't tell anybody that."

I don't know what to say, but that doesn't seem to matter. A strange thought comes into my head as I try to figure out if there's anything I can do to help: it's hard to believe that Brenda and Jake live in the same world, that two people living in this little town can have such different lives. Then again, maybe it's not so hard to believe—my life is totally different from Jake's too; I just don't like to think about that too often.

"My dad broke his hip in a freak accident and had trouble sleeping," she says. "We didn't have medical insurance and the bills kept piling up. He cheaped out on his meds. Then he developed a blood disorder that hurt his ability to recover. It kept getting worse and worse and costing more and more. Before that, he could be . . . He used to strut around and be funny and proud and kind of a dink sometimes . . ."

She smiles when she gets to that last part, but it's gone in a flash. A big pause. Another deep breath. She looks to the sky and continues: "One day he drove off down a dirt road in the middle of nowhere, put a hose in the exhaust pipe, and that was that."

For what seems like the millionth time, I don't know what to say.

"I can remember everything so clearly. The hospital gave us a bag of his clothes. There was still his sweat on his shirt. I'll never forget that. A few years later, when I was around twelve and living at my mom's again, I stole a bottle of wine from the kitchen and I sat in a field and started drinking it and just swore at the sky . . ."

Her voice trails off again.

"I threw up about halfway through the bottle," she says. For an instant, she seems to flash a smile.

"Trent—I saw him just hanging there," she says. "His eyes . . ."

She goes quiet for a while. Her eyes are so big now, and so full of disbelief.

I stay quiet too. What could I add beyond another, "I'm sorry?"

"Trent wouldn't have done that!" she suddenly exclaims. "And if he ever did, he wouldn't have done it so that I would be the one to find him. He wouldn't do that to me . . . And the bruises . . ."

"Bruises?"

"There were bruises . . . and a black eye."

My mind flashes to what I witnessed between Jamie and Trent, and I have to wrestle my thoughts back to the present to focus on what she says next: "I fight. I'm pretty good. I have my red belt in Krav Maga."

I'm a little thrown by the sudden change in the direction of our conversation but it must make sense to her.

She pauses. "Israeli Army self-defense. You'd be surprised how good I am. We practice how to fight back against group attacks, knife attacks, even gun attacks. It's ugly but . . ." Another pause, then: "I'll be a black belt in a year or so. We like to call it 'a hundred ways to boot a guy in the nads.'"

She gives me a crazy smile, as if she knows how goofy that sounds. She giggles a little. Finally, laughter.

There's something safe there. Thank God she still has that.

I get serious again, sort of. "Is there anything I can do? Don't want you hoofing my nads."

She gives me a quick smile.

"Dunno. But it wasn't a suicide. Trent wouldn't do that. He wouldn't." She inhales deeply, the way I would if I was trying not to cry. "He would have known how much it would hurt me."

There's not much to say after that. I don't tell her about the beef between our brothers, even though it might help replace the suicide theory. Not now. Maybe not ever.

Sometime around 3:00 a.m. she brings up Carlito, after we've spent hours drifting from topic to topic—movies we both like, the best place in town to get fish and chips, and trips we've taken to Toronto and farther.

"He offered me a job," she says.

"Job?" I wasn't aware Carlito even worked himself. I'd heard he just hangs around a strip club in East London and acts as a bouncer from time to time. I'm pretty sure he also sells drugs, like quite a few of the younger and shadier Annihilators.

"Yeah. Dancing."

She sees me frown. "Dancing" is code for stripping in my brother's world. In front of half-drunk strangers who either ignore the girls or stare too hard. Either way, I feel sick when I imagine her doing it.

"I turned him down, though—he's asked again."
There's a long pause, as if she's waiting for me to say
something. When I don't, she continues: "He's not all
bad."

I could have lived without that last part.

I'm trying hard not to get sucked into feeling
jealous. I concentrate instead on her. How special
she is. How lucky I am to be sitting here with her on
this night in my car. The world has been waiting for
billions of years for her arrival and I'm the one who
gets to talk to her right now. I need to be happy with
that.

Still, I wonder if I could take Carlito in a fight. It
might come down to how dirty I'm prepared to be.

"We're all just trying to get by," she says and her
voice drifts away.

We must both doze off, because she's leaning
against my shoulder when I wake up and it feels nice.
She awakens with a jolt a few minutes later, and the
conversation winds back to her brother.

"Once they found he could cook it really well—
meth, I mean—they wouldn't leave him alone," she
says. "He learned how to do it from a guy he met in
jail when he was nabbed for shoplifting."

I hadn't heard about Trent being in jail but it
doesn't really surprise me.

"They?"

"Club guys. Annihilators. Spartans. And the big
club, the Popeyes. They all wanted a piece of him. They

all wanted him to work more. Cook more. Teach some guys. But they all wanted to control him too."

I want to ask questions but I keep quiet instead. Maybe she just needs a sounding board right now. Then she steers the conversation elsewhere again. "My mother lost it for a while after Dad died," she says. "She just pulled away. Went cold. Never got right again. At least not for long. Trent took me away to live with some relatives in Sarnia, and ever since then, he hasn't really wanted me living here with Mom. It was nice to be back in town, staying with him, until . . ."

I'm thinking of how Mom might react to losing Jamie as Brenda's voice goes much softer. "Is it so bad to be in my family?" The words are quiet and slow and full of pain. "Are we just a bunch of quitters? Losers?"

I can't help thinking that if it wasn't suicide, it must have been murder. And if it was murder, where does Jamie fit in? I keep thinking about the black eye and bruises.

Brenda's a great girl. I've never felt this way about anyone before, ever.

But Jamie's still my brother.

Chapter 11

In the morning, it's clear to me that I really have to talk with Jamie. I keep trying to convince myself that his argument with Trent wasn't as bad as it looked, but the longer I go without hearing from him, the harder that gets. I'm hoping maybe he'll emerge for Trent's funeral tomorrow.

Bikers are suckers for spectacles, and nothing tops a funeral for one of their pack. A murdered drug dealer might somehow rate an honor guard in black armbands, as if he were a hero who nobly fell during some great crusade. Anything goes at a biker funeral. It's considered totally appropriate to pour booze or toss nickel bags of weed on a coffin as "Born to Be Wild" blares from the speakers. I've even heard of bikers being buried on their Harleys, although I'm pretty sure it's never happened around here. Seems like a waste of a perfectly good motorcycle.

The rest of the day passes in a blur of sleep, trying to catch up with Jamie, and worry—about Jamie and Brenda and Mom and me. I wonder if there will be Popeyes at Trent's service. He wasn't even a full member of the Annihilators, but he did party with the big club and they've been hanging around enough lately.

The next day, I head to the service early, hoping to see Jamie. Just the sight of him would calm me down. I can't see him turning up if he's responsible in any way for Trent's death—Jamie's tough but he's not that cold.

When I get to the cemetery, there's a canopy strung up over a freshly dug grave and a few people standing around it. None of them is Jamie. None of them are bikers. I turn toward the growl of a Harley and see Ripper riding in, alone and wearing his Annihilators vest. In Ripper's worldview, wearing club colors to a funeral is a powerful show of respect. But the fact that he's doing it alone is strange. It's normal for bikers to ride in together in a pack.

They have all sorts of funny thoughts about funerals and death. Some of them call heaven the Forever Chapter. Up there (I'm assuming it's up), they swig bottomless bottles of beer while giving gawkers a perpetual finger. Outlaw bikers often groan that they just want to be left alone, but that's not really true. What's a performer without an audience? In biker heaven, they need civilians to startle in order to make the picture complete.

I guess it shouldn't be surprising that bikers have a love-hate relationship with death, since they often speed up its arrival not just for themselves but for a lot of others too. In their minds, I guess their club status gives them a sort of immortality. They might be plumbers or muffler installers or couriers with ridiculous biker names like Badger, Bam Bam, and Lobo, but they live forever on club websites long after they've stopped bullets or became road pizza.

It's good that Ripper is here. He's the Annihilators' president and the closest thing they have to a wise old man. No one tells Ripper what to do or what not to do. Rumor has it he was plenty tough back in the day, and he apparently has a black belt in something. Lots of bikers tried to rip off his patch back when clubs used to offer a bounty (consisting of a case of beer) to anyone who could hunt down a biker from a rival club and forcibly remove his crest. Apparently, no one ever managed to tear off Ripper's patch, but he ripped off plenty in his time. Is that how he got his nickname? Or maybe it's because he used to rip around on his motorcycle or because RIP is the abbreviation for "rest in peace." Maybe he's called Ripper for all of those reasons. Maybe someday I'll ask.

Ripper's actually a grandfather, although no one has the nerve to call him "Gramps" or "Grandpa" or anything stupid like that. He's a retired ironworker and proud of it. He once told me how cool it is to drive by a building and know you helped put it up.

He must be at least sixty-five, and has a union pension and some sort of other pension from a short stint he did in the military.

"At least we have our privacy," Ripper says to me now.

He's being sarcastic, gesturing toward some of the cops surveilling the scene. It's never a good sign in the biker world when police outnumber mourners at the funeral of someone connected to the club. There are at least a half dozen of them here.

I see Brenda on the other side of the grave, standing next to a very distraught-looking woman. That must be her mother. They're both trying to comfort a pregnant young woman; Trent's girlfriend, I'm guessing. She looks so stunned and lost. I wonder if she even notices the low turnout from the club.

Brenda's wearing a plain black dress that's nothing fancy, but she looks so beautiful—older and sophisticated. Her hair is pulled back tight in a way I've never seen it before. Checking out a girl at a funeral seems a little weird, but I can't help myself; it's hard to look away.

But the sound of a bike distracts me, and I turn to watch, hoping it will be Jamie. My stomach drops as Carlito pulls up on his Harley. He's alone too but he's not wearing his biker colors. He's got on a black dress shirt and black jeans and he looks a bit like a waiter. He ignores me and Ripper and goes straight to Brenda and her family. It surprises me that he thinks it's okay to snub Ripper like that. It wouldn't kill him to be polite to me, either.

Carlito hugs Brenda's mother, as if they know each other. Then he gives Brenda a hug too. It's hard to see if she's hugging him back. Carlito steps back from the grave; so he can't be *that* close to Brenda's family. Still, he makes no effort to walk over and join Ripper and me.

Brenda and her mother are both wearing shades, and I'm sure they've been crying. Brenda's mother looks like an old biker chick. There's something rough about her, and it's not just the four or five earrings she has on one ear. Her skirt is tight across her hips and it's more a style you'd put on for dancing than mourning. She's wearing a black blouse that's not buttoned up as high as you might expect.

She frowns in the direction of the police and doesn't look away when some of them stare back. There's something so raw about the pain in her face that it hurts to even look. Now isn't the time to approach Brenda, I can tell.

Photographers huddle nearby, including one from the *Sun-Sentinel* who's carrying a Nikon and a long lens. He points it at Ripper; it would be rude to step away from him to get out of the shot, so I don't. I'm sure the biker squad already has plenty of photos of Ripper. Some smart cop will notice Carlito and they'll get some fresh ones of him as well. I guess my photo is about to go into some police file.

I can see from Ripper's expression that he's deep into one of his Zen moods and couldn't care less about the news or police cameras. Ripper once insisted that I read this weird old book called *Zen and the Art of Motorcycle Maintenance*. After I realized he wasn't joking, I read a bit of it and it wasn't bad; so far, though, I'm not sure if it's profound or hippy-dippy gibberish. Today, I'm just grateful to have Ripper here so I have someone to stand beside.

"Trollop 'ordered' us not to come," Ripper says.

He smirks for a second. The idea of a regular biker ordering the president to do anything is pretty much unheard of. That would never happen in a bigger club.

"So why'd you come?" I ask.

I know I'm not supposed to dig into club business. As soon as I ask I wonder if he'll get angry.

Instead, he jokes: "I have my own brain. It's creaks a bit when I try to use it but it's all mine."

I apparently don't smile quickly enough at that, so he adds: "I'm more than a hat rack."

Usually, Ripper's more of a smiler than a talker. Today, he seems ready to actually have a conversation. I seize the opportunity.

"Why are you a biker?"

It's such a big, big question, and I don't even know why I asked it. Sometimes I just have trouble shutting up.

"Had to be something."

Classic Ripper-speak. He isn't being rude. I think I get his drift.

He decides to expand a little further. "A lot of it just happened. It wasn't some great plan. We actually rode bikes back then in the sixties. Imagine that? Bikers who ride bikes. We wanted to talk bikes with people who understood what we were about. We wanted to be left alone by pretty well everyone else, except the hippy girls."

Another big pause and then he continues: "No one says 'Hey you' when you're wearing a patch. Drivers are scared to cut you off. When you got your patch, you went from being a nobody to being a rock star, and you didn't have to learn to sing. People gawking at you instead of ignoring you."

"You don't seem to be too crazy about those guys from the Popeyes," I say cautiously.

"Different world now. A patch is just a piece of cloth. It's the man wearing that patch that counts. Just like wearing a black belt doesn't automatically make you a tough fighter." He's smiling now, shifting into the Uncle Ripper role that I love. "It's what you do to deserve your patch that really counts."

"So you don't want to be in the Popeyes or another big club?"

"It's neither here nor there. Buddha is everywhere."

Ripper has a way of screwing with you and being totally honest, all in the same sentence.

"Big clubs bring big police heat," he continues. "Big police projects. Big police funding. More informants. More paid agents. There's more money in being a police informant nowadays than there is in being a drug dealer, not that I'd recommend either line of work."

His face loosens and he shrugs his shoulders. The ceremony is starting. Lesson over.

There are about twenty people at the funeral besides the ones who are obviously police, most of whom I presume to be Brenda's family members or family friends. Brenda doesn't appear to be very close to many of them.

After the service, she approaches me as dirt is shoveled onto her brother's casket. I watch Carlito's eyes following her.

I know I don't have the right words. The perfect ones might come to me later, when life has already moved on, but for now all I can manage is: "Sorry."

Brenda looks off into nowhere.

"Like I said, I know he did some sketchy things, but he was a good guy," she says. "He tried."

The word "tried" sounds particularly raw. She looks over at the not-so-undercover police and a press photographer and then sighs. I'm trying to keep the skepticism out of my expression, but Trent was a meth cook after all. She must sense this, because she continues, "He didn't even want a patch. He deliberately didn't buy a Harley because he wanted them to stop asking him to join. My brother used to say, 'When you're broke, you're a joke.' He didn't want to be a joke. He didn't want me to be one."

I just look at her and she goes on talking. I love her sense of loyalty to her brother, but there's something unreal about all of it.

"He saw I was getting messed up myself. Waking up next to guys like Carlito."

I frown and she sees this, but she doesn't stop. She has no time right now for my delicate little feelings. She's crying again. Not loud. Not dramatic. Not trying for a response from me. Just crying. Really crying. Shaking.

Before I know it I'm touching both of her arms. It's sort of a hug. And it's the first time we've deliberately touched. She doesn't flinch or even acknowledge it. Does she even feel it? As she speaks, her voice is robotic. Stunned.

"I need to know who killed him."

Need.

Her mother gives her a look that's almost like a warning. It's time to go.

"Later," I say.

She nods.

On her way over to her mother, she nods at Carlito too. I feel a flash of resentment even though I know I have no right to feel that way. But I have to wonder: What does she get from him? It's like she has a separate need for each of us.

As I get into the Cruze, I try to figure out why the turnout was so embarrassingly low. It was a deliberate snub. There's no other way to look at it.

Maybe the Annihilators have concluded—rightly or wrongly—that Trent committed suicide. That's the least frightening explanation. Suicides are considered a coward's way out of my brother's world. Die from shooting too much heroin into your veins or driving your bike too fast without a helmet or being too slow on the trigger in a drug rip-off and you're worthy of eternal hero status. Step off a chair with a rope around your neck and they won't acknowledge that you ever walked the face of the earth.

There is a second possible explanation for the snub. In my mind, it's worse than the suicide theory and almost too troubling to consider.

Have the bikers decided that Trent was a rat? If so, it's a safe bet that he was murdered. Anyone of the Annihilators, and even bikers from outside our little backwater town, would have felt justified in killing him. Some of them might have even felt obligated to do it.

Including Jamie.

Chapter

12

A big photo of Trent's funeral appears on the *Sun-Sentinel*'s homepage just hours after I leave the cemetery. Ripper and I are clearly identifiable behind the casket. Ripper is wearing his full Annihilators colors and he looks like a classic biker from head to toe. If it wasn't so unsettling to see myself in the shot, I might have found it pretty cool. I half hoped to see Brenda too. It could have been our first photo together.

The caption identifies Ripper by his real name, Paul Matheson, which isn't really that surprising since he's a local sort-of-celebrity; I'm not identified at all, and I'm grateful for that.

When I rush into the newsroom at the start of my night shift, the city editor looks up at me but keeps his distance. Within twenty minutes I'm settled in, feeling like I'm babysitting the city from the fifth floor with TweetDeck and emergency scanners.

Bill sticks his head into the radio room to say hello. I'm sure he noticed me in the funeral photo. Might he be able to help me figure out what's going on?

"Can I ask you something?" I say. "How do police know when something's a murder and not a suicide?"

"Depends. How did the person die?"

"Found hanging in his home. His garage."

Does my voice crack a little? Can he see something in my eyes?

Bill's a nice guy. He likely already knows what I'm talking about. This is a small enough city and he has plenty of sources besides his cop daughter. It doesn't take Sherlock Holmes to connect the dots here.

"Depends on a bunch of things. Was the person depressed?"

"Don't think so. Stressed, but not actually depressed."

"Had the person attempted suicide before?"

"Don't think so."

"Who bought the rope?"

"Don't know. Why does that matter?"

"Generally, suicide victims don't bother to hide things like that. Why would they? It would be more mysterious if there was no record of the purchase. Was a note left at the scene?"

He has a little rhythm going as he moves through his mental checklist.

"Don't think there was a note."

"Had he been threatened?"

"Not sure. Maybe. He definitely had some bad enemies."

He is looking at my face now, studying my expression.

He has to know what case I'm talking about. This is St. Thomas. There aren't a lot of unsolved homicides.

"Were there injuries to the body?"

"He had a black eye. A big one."

"How do you know?"

"I do."

I'm not about to reveal that Brenda told me, and he doesn't press the issue.

"He had bruises too," I add.

"His family should try to get the autopsy report."

"Wouldn't it be obvious if it was a murder?"

"Not necessarily. It's quite possible to hang someone and make it look like suicide. There are things that the coroner might notice, though. If the neck is broken, you should be really suspicious, because that could have happened before the body was hanged. It's not so hard to do, if you're big or strong enough or there are enough of you. It's the way some pros kill people." He pauses for a beat and then adds, "Some guys in the Popeyes have done it that way. Sometimes . . ."

"Sometimes?"

"Sometimes a murder is a statement. They want the body to be found and for everybody to know it was a murder in order to send a message. In a case like that, they'll just shoot the guy. It's a warning. They want everyone to know that they can kill somebody and then just walk away and carry on with their lives, that they are outside of the law. Other times, they want to fly under the radar. They just want the guy dead. In an instance like that, they might dangle someone from a rafter and make it look like suicide. Depends on their motives, but the victim's just as dead either way."

Brenda's brother was a skinny, relatively short guy. Way smaller than Trollop or Carlito or my brother, and way, way weaker than those juice monkeys from the Popeyes. It would be easy for any of them to have killed him and then made it look like suicide. Who would care, besides his family?

"Was the door locked from either the inside or the outside?" Bill asks.

"Not locked."

Trent was feeling pretty good about life just before he died, according to Brenda. His girlfriend was pregnant and he really wanted to start a family with her. Pretty good reasons to stick around.

My mind flashes to what it must have been like for Brenda when she walked into the garage. Did she check for a pulse? Was it completely obvious that Trent was dead, or did she hold out a tiny bit of hope that he could be saved? Did she think of her dad? Did she remember being a little girl and her brother taking her to Brownies?

I'm getting more and more worried about Jamie. I wonder if Bill can see that on my face.

"I need you to look into something," I say impulsively.

"What?" He looks a little startled. Maybe even annoyed. He's too good a reporter to just do me a favor, and I didn't mean it to sound as abrupt as it did.

"All that stuff I was saying about the guy who was found hanging, that's the Annihilators' meth cook."

Bill doesn't look at all shocked, just interested.

"I'd like to be a source for you. I can tell you that I know for a fact that his body was bruised."

I know I'm crossing a line here. Being a source is a lot like being a rat. But how can telling the truth to a good guy be a bad thing?

"I was already working on it. I like you and believe you but I'd have to ask around. You're not exactly a neutral source. Nothing personal, but I need others."

"That's good. I want that. I'm glad you're asking around. Remember all of those cops at the funeral? Would they be there if they thought it was a suicide?"

Bill shakes his head.

But I haven't told him the worst part—my fear that the killer might be Jamie. I keep pushing that thought out of my mind but it keeps sneaking back in. Maybe Bill already gets it.

I know Brenda deserves to know what happened, and I want to think I can handle the truth. But . . . but . . . what if it's Jamie? If he's convicted of murder, he'll go to prison for a long, long time. Mom will fall apart. And Brenda will be disgusted by me and my family. I'll be alone.

But I'm getting ahead of myself. I've been told that imagining something bad is almost always worse than actually experiencing something bad, but it doesn't feel that way right now. If Jamie stays in the club, and he's already a hit man, what's next? One day it'll be him hanging from a rafter or found dead in a ditch or convicted of another murder. Even if he's guilty of this crime and gets away with it, I don't want to imagine that he could be happy living that way. I don't think I'm betraying him by seeking the truth. He's told me to be true to myself, and I feel I'm trying to save him, to save all of us. I just hope he sees it that way. Looking for the truth seems like the only place to start.

◄○►

The story appears the next day on the *Sun-Sentinel*'s website under the headline "Biker death may be murder, police believe." It's posted around noon. Bill worked quickly.

In the article, Bill notes how police surveillance was out in force at the funeral but had virtually no one to observe or photograph. The conclusion: if the police thought it was a suicide, they wouldn't have shown so much interest in the funeral. The story goes on to reveal that the garage door was unlocked and that Trent's neck was broken. There's also mention of the black eye and the bruising to his body. Bill quotes sources who saw Trent's body or the official reports—

the on-scene paramedics and coroner's office, I'm guessing, since most of the sources aren't identified. He keeps my name out of it. I feel safer trusting him now.

"Investigators are working with the theory that it was a murder staged to look like a suicide," the article concludes. Creepy as that is, it must help make Brenda feel a little bit better.

Murder is awful, but it's still better than suicide. You can at least get mad at a killer. But what if the killer is Jamie? The question still feels unreal. And I feel like a traitor.

I text Brenda immediately after reading the story.

That means a lot, she texts back. *Now we don't look like such losers.*

I'm sure Jamie has read the article too.

I wonder what he's thinking right now.

Chapter 13

Just when it seems like Jamie has dropped off the face of the earth, he pops up in cyberspace as if nothing has happened.

What's up?

The text comes a couple of days after he vanished and Trent's body was found. Somehow, Jamie makes it sound like everything is normal.

Lots, I reply. *Where are you?*

My place, Jamie texts. I'm surprised—and relieved. I've driven by his house several times over the last few days, but he's never been home. I guess he finally is.

Can I come by?

What I have to ask him is too big for texting. I need to be able to see his face when we talk.

Sure.

Jamie lives near the road into town, on a side street close to the Jumbo statue in a cottage-style home with absolutely no charm. I stop by to visit once a month, maybe more, depending on if he's in town and how things are at home with Mom. It's not that unusual for me to spend nights at Jamie's. Sometimes his biker friends drop by when I'm there. They're generally easygoing—not the hotheaded stereotypes you see in movies or on TV.

Jamie's Harley is out front when I get there. He's clearly not hiding from anyone. There's even a red-and-black Annihilators sticker on the gas tank. It's a warning/threat to potential thieves, and in our town, it works way better than a chain or a bike lock.

When I walk in the door, I can tell that Jamie is preoccupied and distracted. He keeps glancing out the window, isn't looking me in the eye. It's not the time to talk. I'll have to wait him out.

He has two cell phones on the table and seems to be watching them intently but pretending not to. This isn't unusual for guys in my brother's crowd: one is meant for business, one for personal stuff. By business, I mean criminal business. At least I think I do. I don't know exactly what Jamie's involved in these days and I don't particularly want to know. I'm not into drugs and he doesn't push anything on me. Still, I imagine Jamie is mixed up in the biker drug trade on some level. I can't see him being into extortion, but who knows?

Sports highlights are playing on the TV as I scramble eggs and fry up sausages for dinner. I put a plate down in front of Jamie, but his mind is clearly somewhere else. I'm used to his moods by now, but tonight feels different: we're both tense. The TV's blaring but he's still watching his phones; whatever he's expecting has his full attention. And he's not sharing.

We eat together in silence. I'm sure he thinks he's doing me a favor by not telling me whatever's on his mind. Eventually I crash on the couch with the TV tuned to *Forensic Files* while he retreats into his bedroom. I'm asleep within minutes.

Baaaam!

I'm sound asleep on the couch, with the TV still on, when I hear it. I'm groggy, but no one could sleep through this.

Baaaam!

This time the sound is even louder and feels like it could knock the house down.

Tiny sparkles fill the air with what looks like pixie dust, adding to my confusion.

"Get on the floor!" A man's voice, deep and threatening. "Now! Lie down on the floor! Now!"

Sparkles are everywhere.

The man doing the shouting is standing in the semi-darkness amid the glittering dust, a crazy silhouette. A half dozen other men in helmets surround him, looking more like big ants than humans.

Jamie's emerged from the bedroom and is standing a few feet behind me. I can hear him inhale deeply, trying to get his breathing under control. He too suffered from anxiety attacks when he was around my age, long before he got control of his stammer and started acting cool and tough.

I've never had a gun pointed at me and now, all at once, there are several.

I'm in shock as I drop to the floor and lie face down. Moments later, I'm stuck in the back of a police cruiser with handcuffs around my wrists.

Jamie is led out a few minutes after me, and I watch as he's ushered into the back of another cruiser. I look at him in disbelief through the car window. I would have expected to feel more emotion in this situation, but right now I just feel like I'm watching a bad movie in the middle of the night. And Jamie? He doesn't seem worried at all; in fact, he looks relieved—*really* relieved. I think about this and realize it makes sense: if it had been angry bikers bursting into his home, he'd be bleeding on the floor right now, not sitting in the back of a police car.

Jamie and I are separated from the time we leave his place and no one feels the need to update me about what's going on. At the police station, I am placed in a cell alone. The walls are concrete, painted a dull gray. There's a toilet with no seat in the corner of the room. Privacy and comfort mean nothing here.

"Where's Jamie?" I ask.

The guard doesn't reply.

A while later, a plainclothes detective comes down to see me. He walks right into my cell and sits down on the bed to talk, clearly not considering me any kind of a threat. I recognize him as the father of one of the backup tackles on the football team.

"Son, this is serious," he tells me. "We're looking at your brother in a murder investigation."

"A murder?" I try to act shocked. "Who?"

"Trent Wallace."

"Am I being charged with something?"

"No."

I am starting to get a little angry. I'm already a lot afraid.

He changes the subject. "How's the leg?" Obviously, he recognizes me too, but I don't feel like jock talk right now.

"I need to call my mom."

He hands me his cell phone.

I punch in Mom's number; she is short with me when she answers.

"Josh. I'm at work . . ."

"I've been picked up by the police. So has Jamie . . ."

There's a long pause and I can almost see the panic on her face.

"Why?" she finally asks, the frightened tone coming through loud and clear. I hate hearing her voice like this but I have no choice—I have to tell her.

"I don't know. I haven't been charged with anything. I think I was just brought in for questioning because I was at his place. But Jamie . . ."

There's a long pause on the line.

"What's it about?"

"They think he's mixed up in a murder."

"Murder?"

The word comes out like a gasp. There must be people around her. The phone goes silent on her end. Then I hear a big sigh. She starts to cry, gently at first and then it picks up steam.

"Who?" she finally asks.

"They say it was Trent . . . a guy sort of with the club."

More silence, then: "I know who he is. I can get off work."

I wonder what she'll tell them. Family emergency? I spend the next half hour making small talk with the cop who asked about my leg. He sounds concerned about my football future, but I'm not sure if he's playing me or if he's sincere.

Mom is shaking as she comes into the police station. It's late, and I'm ready to go home. I never was charged with anything. I wonder if she's going to give me some big sloppy hug. Instead, she walks super-rigidly and stares off into space.

"I'll drive," I say.

She ignores me and addresses the cop who's leading me out of the cell.

"I need to see my son," she tells him. She doesn't say Jamie's name, but she's obviously not talking about me.

She's trying so hard to sound together.

"I'm afraid you can't at the moment." I appreciate that the cop's polite to her.

"Why?"

"He's speaking with some other officers."

That sounds so much nicer than "he's a murder suspect." Still, Mom looks shocked. She just goes quiet. This is for real. Her boy is being interrogated about a murder and there's not a thing she can do about it.

"I'll drive," I say again.

Mom hands me the keys and we walk quietly out of the station. I check the paper's website on my phone before I get into the car. The raid has already been reported: a short, uninspired effort that takes up a half-dozen paragraphs, below a dramatic "BREAKING NEWS" banner.

The report reads as if it's based on a police press release and is headlined, "Biker murder suspect arrested at gunpoint." The sub-headline reads, "Teen released from suspect's house."

The story begins, "A local biker has been charged with murder after another local man was found dead in his garage." There's a photo of Jamie, looking blankly into the camera. If I didn't know him, I'd think he was guilty. It's the biggest crime story to hit this town in years; I have to take some deep breaths and walk around a little before I can read on. Trent is called "a known associate of the Annihilators

Motorcycle Club" while Jamie is identified as "a long-standing full patch member of the club."

Even though I'm not named in the story since I'm a minor, I can't imagine how it could be worse. Jamie could be heading off to prison for life. Our family name is mud. We don't have much money for a lawyer. In truth, we don't really have any money for a lawyer. And Brenda? I wonder if she's ever going to talk to me again. I have to sit still for a moment and fight the urge to throw up.

As I'm starting the car, Jake texts me. He's obviously read the article too and he's worried.

Can I help?

That's so Jake, so naive. What could he possibly do? Get his mother to bake the cops and the bikers a plate of cookies each and make everyone promise never to be bad again? But it's not his fault that he can't understand this world that I live in.

I'll let you know but thanks, I text back.

Don't be a stranger, he says.

I sense that Jake is scared, like he's on the verge of losing something too.

Chapter
14

As I drive home, I can't shake the picture in my head: Jamie in jail, feeling lost and confused and frightened but trying to look tough and in control. I saw that face a lot before he finally moved out of the house back when I was in grade three. I wonder if his stammer is starting up again.

Mom's clearly imagining things too.

"I have to go see him," she says.

"Huh?"

"Doesn't he have to have a bail hearing?"

She's right. What does she think she'll do? Order the guards to treat him nicely?

"Mom, trust me, you don't want to go."

"I have to. You don't . . ."

Jamie's almost thirty. He's not a little boy anymore, except in her eyes.

"I'll go instead, okay? Please. There's nothing you can do, Mom. At least not right now."

I really don't need her breaking down or freaking out in public.

"But . . . ," she says.

"I'll go. Trust me, it's best for you and him if you stay away for now. You know he'll be embarrassed. It's so public. You can have a private visit with him soon."

Part of me can't even believe we are having this conversation, talking about my brother's bail hearing and visiting him in jail. I should be in my own little cocoon, lifting weights and working on my future. It's not like I have a lot of time to get ready for football season. But this is right now, and there won't be much left of my family if this goes south. I go on: "There could be reporters there. You don't want your picture in the paper."

"I don't care."

"Jamie would care."

She knows I'm right. As I plead with her, it dawns on me that I'm in a bit of a dicey position. What if the editors at work tell me to do some horrendous "I know him" story? Or want to interview me for a piece about the club? I don't need the job that badly. What I do know is that this is my time to step up and do something. I just wish I had a clue what that was.

Chapter
15

I catch a bit of sleep in preparation for what's going to be a tough day. How do I prepare for Jamie's bail hearing and the sight of him in the prisoners' box? I keep waking up in the night, asking painful what-ifs. What if Jamie and the rest of the bikers follow their no-ratting rule? Then no one will cooperate with the police, even to exonerate my brother, and Jamie faces the very real threat of being sent off to a life sentence in prison for murder, even if he's innocent. That means twenty-five years without parole.

Jamie's not perfect, but murder? I can vaguely imagine him killing someone in self-defense, but I can't see him making a plan to execute anyone in cold blood. I also can't see him staging a crime scene the way Trent's was, but how well do I really know him? He only gives me carefully edited glimpses into his life.

One thing is for sure: I'm in a unique spot to dig out the truth about what happened to Trent. I might only be seventeen, but I think I know the people in the club better than the cops—I've been around them for half of my life—and maybe even better than Bill. Maybe Brenda can help me too—if she's still talking to me after Jamie's arrest. She must know plenty of things I don't, especially about the meth trade.

Even though it's the last place I really want to go, I decide to cruise by the clubhouse. I have a little time before Jamie's 2:15 p.m. appearance in bail court and maybe I'll pick up some clues. There's no way my brother will get bail today but they have to start the process. I wouldn't mind some advice from a real lawyer rather than the free one provided by the court, but Mom and I can't afford that and Jamie's apparently broke too. Maybe the club can help. Ripper's the guy I want to talk to there.

There's always something creepy about the clubhouse, even on a good day, and this definitely isn't a good day. When I pull up, I see Carlito standing outside, talking with the big guy from the Popeyes I saw going into the diner a few days ago. I don't know why they'd be together. I don't know Carlito that well and I don't trust him at all, and the Popeye genuinely scares me. It creeps me out to think Jamie spends time with guys like this, his "bros."

I'm his real brother.

Carlito spots me and nods.

"What's up?" he says.

The Popeye just stares. No smile. No nod.

"Hoping to find Ripper," I say.

"He's not here," Carlito replies. A pause and then, "Too bad about your brother."

I don't tell them that I'm here because sometimes the club jumps in and helps set members up with experienced lawyers. For most charges, like drunk driving and assaults and petty drug things, members are expected to pay up and keep things straight with the lawyers. For big cases that could affect the entire club or its reputation, the president has the power to activate an emergency legal fund.

I heard that once, before I was born, Trollop was suspected of murder but he was never charged. The victim was a friend of the club who was suspected of shooting a cop. The cop was supposedly crooked. It's all part of the Trollop legend, which I suspect is mostly self-created. Who knows what's true? The story is that Trollop's victim wouldn't stop hanging around the clubhouse and bringing police heat to the other bikers. So Trollop supposedly shot him and placed his body in a field near Trollop's barn. As Trollop tells it, the cops were lenient with him after that out of gratitude. Whatever the truth is, the murder was never solved.

"Stay in touch," Carlito says as I hightail it back to the Cruze.

It could be an attempt at friendliness, but somehow it sounds more like a threat.

Chapter
16

Someone from our family should be at Jamie's bail appearance, and I'm all there is. Dad's AWOL and Mom doesn't need to see her eldest boy looking frazzled and unshaven, sandwiched between wife-beaters and drunks. Besides, it wouldn't do Jamie any good to see Mom looking lost and distraught and beaten down by life, just like she did on the day he punched out Dad.

I slip onto a bench in the back, four rows behind the reporter from the *Sun-Sentinel*, who doesn't look in my direction. Just as well. I don't want to talk with anyone and I don't want to be seen either.

I feel both ashamed and strangely protective as Jamie is led into the courtroom by a uniformed guard. He's prisoner number three in a string of bleary-eyed losers who remind me of a row of fish hanging from one of those chains anglers use to hold their catch, before they knock them on the head and gut them.

His eyes dart about the courtroom. I'd hoped someone from the club would show up to support him. It's frowned upon to wear club colors in court, since that just excites the judge and the cops and intimidates potential witnesses. But it wouldn't kill a few bikers to put on street clothes, cover their tattoos, and turn up to let Jamie know they're thinking of him. But no one else is here for him. No boss. No girlfriend. No club brothers. No parent. Just me.

Jamie gives me a little nod and then lowers his eyes. He's trying to look cool, and is standing stiffly with his shoulders back, but I know it's just an act. After about twenty minutes, and cases involving a drunk driver and an unruly john who argued too loudly with a prostitute, I hear our family name called. I've never felt less proud.

The public defender taps Jamie on the elbow and he stands up.

"Does the prosecution oppose bail?" the judge asks.

"Yes, Your Honor," the prosecuting attorney replies. "Most certainly. Due to the severity of the charges and the fact that the accused is part of an organized criminal group."

Organized criminal group! They might break the law here and there but no one ever called the Annihilators organized. The hungover schoolteacher and the scruffy john who are chained to Jamie both shoot him impressed looks. He's the top fish on their little chain now. I wonder if it made the prosecutor feel tough to say "organized criminal group," like he'd just bagged El Chapo or a modern-day Al Capone.

"We need to keep the accused in custody," the prosecutor says.

"Need?" the judge asks. He is considerably more animated now than he was during the two previous cases, which had all the drama of someone returning a pair of slippers to Costco.

The prosecutor and the judge seem collegial, almost friendly. It's easy to picture them going out for a beer and a few laughs once the workday is over.

"For reasons that will become abundantly clear in the fullness of time," the prosecutor says. This just sounds pompous to me.

"Excuse me?" the judge says.

"Let's just say we don't wish to interfere with police operations, and we also certainly don't wish to endanger anyone connected with the police," the prosecutor replies.

"Anyone connected?" the judge asks.

"Yes, Your Honor," the prosecutor says. "Suffice it to say, police have ongoing operations and operatives to consider. This is a first-degree murder trial, after all." He pauses for dramatic effect. "A first-degree murder trial involving figures associated with organized crime."

It sounds like the prosecutor has just admitted in open court that they have an informant, maybe more than one, working for their side. Is he making this stuff up? Is he hinting that Jamie would go after the informant and harm him or her if he's released on bail? That's what it sounds like. Or is he hinting that Jamie might become an informant himself?

I can't believe what I'm hearing. Rats die in my brother's world. Maybe he's just trying to throw a scare into Jamie, or maybe he's just plain stupid, but I don't see how anyone could be that dumb and hold such an important job. I'm glad I'm sitting down because otherwise I think my knees would buckle. I'm shocked yet again when I notice that the big guy from the Popeyes has slipped into the courtroom and is now sitting in the back row. He must have heard everything.

Jamie sees the Popeye and his face tenses up even more.

Maybe the out-of-town guy is wondering if Jamie will turn rat now that the pressure is on. I've heard that powerful bikers have ways of getting at people behind bars. I have the feeling that Jamie's life has just been put in even more danger.

I want to slap my brother right now. How could he get himself into this mess? Our coach sometimes tells us, "Tell me who your friends are and I'll tell you who you are." If that's true, what does all of this say about

Jamie? He was a role model for me, back when he was a football player himself, but now . . .

According to the coach, there's a positive in every situation, if you just try hard enough to find it. All I can see right now, though, is Jamie being led out of the courtroom, still in custody, looking lost and afraid.

Chapter
17

The next morning, I get to the jail almost an hour before visiting hours begin. A few other people are already waiting on the metal benches just inside the main doors by the reception desk. It's only a day and a half after the arrest, and I could use a break from police and guards and bikers. But Jamie's my brother and you don't abandon your brother, I tell myself.

Visitors have to be buzzed in through the front door and they only take a dozen or so at a time. Signs in the reception room let us know that we are being recorded on camera. Everyone keeps to themselves, either embarrassed or sullen or a bit of both. None of us can act too superior under these circumstances. One by one, we pass our identification through a slot in the thick Plexiglas wall of a guard's booth. A teenager ahead of me in line doesn't have any ID and just leaves, pulling his headphones on and trying to keep his swagger.

The guard behind the Plexiglas asks about my relationship to Jamie, then I'm handed a key for a locker that's just a few feet away. I drop off my keys and cell phone and pens and loose change and everything else I have that contains metal, including my belt.

I am wearing an old purple and gold Golden Ghosts' football jersey with my number on it—51. I didn't put it on as any big statement, but it does feel comforting. My brother likes to wear his club colors to prop himself up and I suppose I'm doing the same. Different game, same feeling.

Next, I'm directed through a door controlled by buzzers to a holding room decorated with grim posters, bearing images of things like syringes accompanied by the helpful statement "Your lifestyle could be the death of you."

A woman who looks like she's in her thirties sits on a bench near two school-aged boys who somehow seem to think it's normal to be here. The younger of the pair is reading a book called *500 Amazing Things* while his older brother works earnestly on a tablet. A couple of the women on another bench are trying to look hot, their brightly colored bras peeking out from too-tight blouses. The overall effect is more valiant than sexy. Near them sits a good-looking but somehow scary girl who's about nineteen. She has two long blond pigtails, and she looks like a super-tough Heidi, someone you don't want to make angry.

Such loser lives. Convict family lives. I like to think we're not there yet, that we'll never get there. When I was a little kid, Jamie made me feel proud and safe. When did things change so much?

I wonder if anyone else in the room has a family member facing the kind of sentence Jamie could be looking at. If he's convicted, I'll be spending a lot more time in places like this. At some point, maybe it'll start to feel normal for me too.

I'm not sure what kind of a reception to expect from Jamie. I know he doesn't really want me to see him here. I love my brother, but I can't remember the last time I actually said that to him. He's not that affectionate either, to be honest, but right now I sort of wish things were different.

Jamie has to be feeling humiliated. Underneath all the biker swagger, he has a pretty thin skin, and it must be hard to convince yourself that you're a winner when you've just been paraded from a cell into a courtroom and then back again.

There's another set of buzzed doors to get through, but first we all have to get wanded like at the airport. Finally I'm walking down a hallway toward the visiting room. At a couple of points, through the windows, I can see a tiny enclosed green space with a bench. Grass seems oddly out of place here with all the swirls of razor wire.

I sit on one of a dozen stools in the room where I will actually get to see my brother, albeit through

Plexiglas. I notice that the stools are all bolted to the floor.

There are a couple of sterilizing stations meant for cleaning the phones that we'll use to talk to the people we're visiting, but a middle-aged woman in a "Kiss the boys and make them die" T-shirt grumbles that one of them is out of soap. The cinder block walls are painted a wimpy institutional blue that is so inoffensive it's actually offensive, in a denial-of-life kind of way.

At last, Jamie is led into the room on the other side of the Plexiglas. Everyone on the prisoners' side looks ridiculous and guilty in their orange jumpsuits, like a mutant cross between Krusty the Clown and the Boston Strangler. Jamie is still trying to look cool and in control as he settles down on his stool.

"They treating you okay?" is what I start with.

He shrugs and says nothing. He knows when I get nervous I talk too much and can say amazingly inappropriate things. But what's the right thing to say when your big brother could be facing a life sentence for murdering the older brother of the girl of your dreams?

I try not to hear the conversations happening around us but I can't help it. A woman is crying. A man beside her is angry. Another prisoner passes behind Jamie and taps him on the shoulder. Jamie turns and smiles. They fist bump and nod and the other man walks away. My brother already has jailhouse "bros."

Jamie looks at the team jersey I'm wearing and for a second his mind seems to drift away. I remember Dad taking me to watch him play when I was little. Jamie seemed like such a superstar, and I was so proud to be his brother. I even taped his number, 38, on a T-shirt to wear to his games. That seems like so long ago.

"What do you do in there?" I ask.

"Play cards. Bridge mostly. Might learn how to play chess." A quick smile, like he's somehow in control of the situation. Like everything's okay. Like he planned for things to turn out like this.

"I know you didn't do this," I blurt out, hoping he'll confirm it, say it's all a big mistake. Instead, Jamie looks startled for a moment, then regains his composure. He doesn't answer me. He just looks down.

"How can I help?" I plead.

Jamie's tone changes immediately. His voice is no longer flat and casual. He's clearly angry.

"Stay out of it."

He glares at me. There's no hint of warmth to him now.

I want to scream back, "How can you do this to me? How can you do this to Mom? It's our name too! We have lives too! Do you realize you're hurting all of us? Who are you to give me orders?"

Right now, I can't believe I ever looked up to Jamie.

Can't he understand that Mom'll snap if he goes to prison? And who's going to take care of her if he ends up behind bars? It'll have to be me.

The woman on my right is sobbing loudly now, and it's tough not to turn my head and tell her to shut up.

"I heard a guy in here last week had his ear cut off."

There's a little hiccup in his voice at the word "guy," but he doesn't look all that unsettled. Why would he tell me this? Am I supposed to be impressed? Or find this funny? It's hard to believe this is the same Jamie who took me to Cub Scouts and swimming lessons. But I decide to play along.

"With what?"

"Porcelain knife."

"How did they do it?"

"Slowly, I'd imagine."

He smirks for just a second, but I can tell he's creeped out too. Is he wondering what sort of a person belongs in a crazy place like this? Then he just shrugs and adds: "They flushed it."

I want to ask Jamie what he knows or suspects about Trent's murder. I want him to help me understand, but I keep reminding myself that our conversation is being recorded. And I'm sure there are plenty of things about Trent's death he won't tell me anyway.

I know in my brother's world solid people, the ones who are respected, just mind their business and do their time when they have to. They don't peek or eavesdrop or gossip or say things that might be overheard. Jamie's goal right now is to be solid, not to fight for his freedom. But someone has to. I have to.

"I want to do something," I say.

"You deaf?"

That comes off as rude, and that's how he wants it to sound. He glares at me again. A pause. He can see my feelings are hurt. His tone softens a little: "Let the lawyer handle things."

Jamie immediately realizes how stupid this sounds. The club hasn't said they're springing for a good attorney. The public defender is overworked and will hardly be Jamie's best advocate. I have to wonder: What kind of a loser breaks the rules and still winds up with next to nothing?

Jamie can see my mind is turning.

"Want to really do me a favor?" he asks. "Seriously?"

"Yeah, definitely."

"Rehab your leg. Be a star. Make lots of tackles. Get that scholarship. Make Mom proud. Make *me* proud."

He finally smiles and reminds me of the big brother I used to know, before he started hanging around with guys with names like "Bear" and "Four-by-Four." Is he afraid I'll turn out like him if I don't get a scholarship and get out of town? Jamie still seems to think he can just give me advice. It's maddening but kind of sweet too. He's still protective of me and Mom, even though he's caused us so much stress over the years—never more so than now.

"Don't just dance with that girl from Trollop's party. Marry her!" He's happy now, at least for the moment. "You're a lousy dancer anyway." He's embarrassing me a little and enjoying it. "Have lots of babies. Start a little tribe of football players. Hopefully they'll look like her, not you. I'll pray for that."

He does have charm, my brother.

I don't remind him that that girl is the little sister of the man he's accused of murdering. Or that Brenda and I have never even held hands, let alone kissed.

"Sounds like a plan" is the best I can do.

He's such a nice guy right now, but I know nice people can do very bad things, just like bad people can do nice things. Once I saw Trollop rescue a caterpillar that found itself inside his house. He carried it outside and placed it on a leaf so it could be free. I imagine Trollop took credit for every butterfly that flew past his window after that.

"Stay out of it," Jamie says again.

His tone has changed in a flash.

Is he afraid I might be in danger too?

Whatever the case, something about the look on his face makes me want to run and hide.

Chapter
18

I haven't gotten any sleep today so it's going to be a tough night shift. I keep picturing Jamie in jail, trying to play it cool when he must be scared out of his mind. I'm beat, and I could use a break, but I don't expect to get it tonight. At least I should be able to do some research on the Popeyes during my shift. The *Sun-Sentinel* has access to some really good databases.

I don't know exactly what I'm looking for, but I know I need to know more. Who is that big Popeye I keep bumping into, the one who makes the Annihilators so nervous? I'm also not sure how the Spartans fit into things. I can't shake the feeling that they're an important part of this puzzle. Their hometown, London, isn't that far away, and while they might be a small club, they're not timid.

I'm trying to draw on what I've learned in football.

Our coaches are big on getting us to define our goals. Then we map out a plan to achieve them. It's not enough to want something. You have to work for it.

What I want in life is so simple, but it feels so far away. Sometimes, late at night, I imagine that I'm the father in a family like Jake's, a family where everyone is relaxed and loving and joking and where things don't always seem on the verge of breaking into pieces. That's my vision of success. Right now, though, I'd settle for my brother not being stuck in prison for the next quarter-century.

I get to work early, and on my way in, I see Bill, who's on his way out.

"The prosecutor at the bail hearing said that there was some sort of police agent or informer," I say. "I don't get it. Why would they say something like that?"

"You need to stay out of that," he tells me. His face has changed since the last time we talked about this; I have never seen him so serious before.

"But . . ." I'm sick of everyone treating me like I'm a kid.

"Seriously."

He's in no mood for an argument and he doesn't seem to want to talk. He sweeps out the door, and a few minutes later, I'm at my workstation, ready to see what I can find on the databases. But there's a note waiting for me, telling me to go and see the city editor. I haven't talked to him since I was hired.

As I walk into his office I can see he has his "serious editor" face on.

"I understand you were at bail court," he says. It sounds a bit like an accusation. I wonder if he's also seen the photo of me at Trent's funeral.

"Yes."

"Your brother?"

"Yes."

There's something judgmental in his tone. I want to swear at him but instead I stare at a point on the wall, just above his right shoulder. He was a crime reporter himself long ago, I've heard, and I imagine he already knows I was at Jamie's house when the arrest took place.

"It's going to be a major story around here."

"Yes."

"It'll attract reporters from out of town."

"Yes."

"Shouldn't you have told us about your conflict here?"

"Conflict?"

"Conflict of interest. Your brother's charged with murder."

"Umm . . . It all happened really quickly."

Thanks, Jamie. Now I'm in trouble just for being your brother.

The city editor's tone softens. "You have a lot to deal with right now."

He's trying to act more like a friendly uncle now and less like a school principal. It's an improvement but still awkward.

"Yes."

I'm surprised at how weak my voice sounds.

"Is your mom okay?"

Where's this coming from? Does everyone know I have a screwed-up home life?

"Yes, thanks."

I'm not about to open up to him. I can't talk here about how Mom seems ready to freak, and how I'm barely holding it together. And I definitely won't talk about Brenda. The *Sun-Sentinel* pays me but they don't own me.

He continues in a kind tone: "I think it might be best if you take a little leave until this cools down. Spend some more time with your family when they need you."

What does he mean by my family? All I have is Mom and she's not home that much. But I'm not about to beg. I could use the money but I guess I can always do some construction work as a day laborer if things get tight. Right now, Jamie is my priority.

Jamie and Trent. And Brenda. And Mom.

And me.

"I'm not firing you. It's just a leave. There's a difference. You understand that?"

"Yes." My tone clearly suggests that I don't.

"There'll be a job for you here once this cools down."

If this cools down. And once football season starts, I won't have time for this place anyway. If I turn pro someday, the *Sun-Sentinel* will be begging to interview me, not railroading me out of a job.

He stands up, which is his way of saying the meeting is over. He leans over to shake my hand, which feels a little formal. I'm not sure what just happened. Was he trying to be helpful or was this just the first step in making sure I never worked here again?

Chapter
19

The last couple of days haven't been great.

I spent the night in the police station, saw my big brother led into court in handcuffs to face a murder charge, then got placed on an indefinite leave from my job, which feels a lot like I just got fired. I also haven't had a chance to talk with Brenda yet. And I imagine Mom will be a mess when I see her. The one bright spot is that I will get to bed earlier than I had expected. Pulling a night shift would have been brutal today.

But when I get home, I have to park on the street because there's a Harley in the driveway in my usual spot. It looks familiar. There's a sinking feeling in the pit of my stomach that I'm trying hard to ignore. As I walk into the house, I see a pair of silver-tipped black cowboy boots by the front door. I glance to the left and there's Carlito on the couch, sipping a beer with his shirt partly unbuttoned.

"Hey bro," he says, smiling like he totally belongs here, not bothering to stand up.

I don't trust myself to speak, so I just give him a brief nod. It's all I can do to keep a lid on things. What the hell is he doing in my house, sitting on the couch like he owns the place?

I'm trying to figure out how to handle the situation when Mom comes down the stairs—and everything clicks. She's in a nightgown. Her hair is messy. She's barefoot. She obviously didn't hear me come in, and she jumps back a little when she sees me. It takes a lot to embarrass her, but I can see that right now, she'd rather be anywhere but here. I know how she feels.

"You two know each other," she finally says.

Somehow this makes things even worse.

"We do," Carlito says. He sounds amused.

I say nothing.

"I should probably be running along," he says after some awkward silence.

He takes a final swig of his beer and puts the can down on the coffee table. He couldn't look more pleased with himself.

There's an unwritten rule among bikers that prohibits sleeping with another member's old lady. But there's no rule that I've heard of against sleeping with another biker's mother. Maybe no one—even in the biker world—ever thought it would be an issue.

A minute later, Carlito's slipping on his boots and

heading out the door. At least there's no show of affection between him and Mom as he leaves; I'm not sure I could take that. She just nods her head at him, and he gives her a smile and a nod.

Moments later, there's the sound of his Harley roaring away.

I don't know what to say. She has never invited bikers into our home before—at least not that I know of.

"Really?" is the best I can muster.

"I thought you were working," she replies in a weak voice.

"I'm going to bed," I say, a little sharply.

Mom looks distraught, but I'm not up to a conversation. I don't want to say anything I'll regret. And that rules out pretty much everything I'm thinking. I'd like to kill Carlito right now, and I'm not the violent one in the family.

The last words I hear from Mom as I head up to the attic are a plaintive, "Why don't you want me to be happy?"

I get it that Mom's an adult and single and human.

I get it that Dad is long gone from her life.

I get it that they should never be together again.

I get it that maybe they never should have been together in the first place.

I get that I'm not perfect myself.

I get all that.

But Carlito?

There's no way that Mom can know about Carlito and Brenda—the history they obviously have. But Carlito didn't seem at all surprised to see me here, so clearly he knows exactly who he was with tonight. Couldn't he have stayed away from our mother?

I stomp up the stairs to my room, grateful for the relative dark and silence of the attic. My mind is reeling. I can't believe Jamie chooses to hang around with guys like this. Or that he would consider risking his freedom for them. What does he get from it? What do they give him that we can't? And now it seems like my mom seeks them out too. Maybe she always has and I've just been too blind to see it. It's like I'm the freak of the family for being sort of normal.

I don't know what, if anything, I can ever say to Mom about this. I also don't know what, if anything, I can say to Brenda. But right now, I can't let myself flip out. I need to focus on freeing Jamie. He's still my brother and he's still facing a murder charge. That can't wait. And it's not like I know what to do about the rest of it anyway.

In the morning maybe I can hit the gym and try to burn this out of my brain, but I seriously doubt there's a workout intense enough to get the job done.

Chapter
20

Hoping you can make it to the captain/coaches BBQ on Sunday, July 30. How's the rehab going?

It's a text from the team's defensive coach and the first thing I read when I get up the next morning. That coach is the one who got me the job at the paper. I'm sure he asks the editor, his buddy, how I'm doing every now and then. I can only imagine what he would have heard if he asked today.

That's not what his message is about, though. Every year, the football team's coaches and captains have a barbecue a couple of weeks before training camp opens. This one's three weeks down the line. By then things might be magically sorted out with Jamie and I might be focused on football again. Or maybe they'll have spun totally out of control and Jamie will be on his way to prison.

Looking forward to it, I reply. It's not a lie. More like wishful thinking. *Rehab's pretty much done. Back*

*in the weight room pretty hard now. Doing some sprints
too.*

*Good man. Make sure you stretch a lot, especially
before and after the sprinting. Don't rush it.*

Thanks. I won't.

Many other guys from the team working out with you?

*My gym's not so big with the guys. Jake's there a lot,
though. We work out together.*

How's he doing?

*Bigger than last year. Quite a bit stronger. Working
hard. Intense.*

The coach knows we're buddies, but it's true. Jake's
not lazy. I leave out the muscle-beach posing and the
rest of Jake's nonsense.

*Good. It's the year for him to step up. Claim a start-
ing spot. Tell him I said that.*

I will.

*We're looking at subbing you in at fullback along
with defensive end. It'll boost our offense and give scouts
another reason to look at you.*

Appreciate it. Can you email me an offensive playbook?

Will do.

Under normal circumstances, this would be amazing news. I'd brag to Mom and Jamie about being one
of the few kids playing both offense and defense. But
today, it doesn't seem to mean that much.

How's other stuff? Your brother? You okay?

There it is. I was hoping we could get through this
chat without Jamie coming up.

It's nice that he's concerned, but I can't chitchat with him about this. I don't like small talk at the best of times, and it's impossible to talk about this in a casual way. A murder beef is hard to joke off.

Not as bad as it looks. It sounds lame but what else can I say? *No fun though.*

It's your time to focus. Next few months determine a lot.

I know he means well, but today I'm easily irritated. I don't need him pressuring me.

I know. I'm working hard.

I'm serious. We all make our choices. Step away from this. We need our captains to be focused. Everyone looks to them for direction.

What is this about? Step away? Did he just give me a pep talk or deliver a threat?

His words just hang there for a while. You can't tell your coach to mind his own business. But still . . .

You're a winner. Keep it that way.

Is that a shot at Jamie? If so, he can take his concern and stick it . . . Or maybe I'm getting too sensitive. It hits me that except for Jake, no one from the team has contacted me about my brother and the jam he's in. I've tried not to think about it too much, but it's still in the back of my mind.

Thanks for info about BBQ, I text him tersely. *See you there. Gotta go. Bye.*

I put my phone back in my pocket and take a deep breath.

Chapter 21

*H*ow *have you been?*

It's a message from Bill Taylor at the paper.

I've barely finished with the coach and here we go again. How do I answer? Fine, except my brother is charged with murdering the brother of the girl that I can't live without? Or perhaps: Today I learned that my mom is sleeping with the biker who used to sleep with my girlfriend and I'd like to kill him? How about: Fine, except that I suspect my girlfriend—okay, she doesn't know she's my girlfriend—might be using that biker to find out who killed her brother? Well, okay, maybe I don't have any evidence of that, and it's a little paranoid to be so suspicious. But there was something about what I saw between Brenda and Carlito at the funeral that bugs me, that's not paranoia.

And what about the idea that was tossed out at the bail hearing about a potential rat in my brother's crowd? Rumors like that get people killed. And turn others into killers. Maybe that's happened already.

Do I tell Bill how what's left of my family would fall apart if my brother goes to prison? Or do I just keep my game face on and try to hang on to some pride?

Fine. And you? I reply.

Wondering how you are.

At this point, figuring out who killed Trent isn't just important for Jamie and his future; it will help hold my life together too. Right now, I need to be lost in something. Alcoholics drown themselves in booze to escape reality. I'll immerse myself in the work of finding answers.

There's a guy from the Popeyes who showed up a while ago, I reply. *I think he has something to do with my brother's mess.*

Do you really want to get into this?

He's talking to me like a source, warning me.

I have to. I don't see how things can get worse.

They can. Trust me, they can. These guys are good at that.

I'm not about to ask him what he means by that. Instead I type, *I don't believe my brother did it. But it looks like he did. He's an easy target.*

Okay.

My brother's no angel but he's not some gangland killer. Wouldn't I know that?

I'm sure that prisons everywhere are full of people whose families think they were framed or got misled by bad apples or were in the wrong place at the wrong time—but still, I just can't believe Jamie did what he's accused of.

So what can I do?

If you can just ask around with your sources. It's a good story, isn't it?

Sure. I'm doing that now anyway and will keep on it, but please don't get yourself in a mess. This isn't football. This is really rough. There's no referee or penalty for not playing nice.

I don't know how to reply. I know this isn't a game, but football doesn't seem like a game to me either; when I'm training or on the field, it's serious. And it's the only thing I really know, my only basis for comparison.

Let's talk soon, he types. *But be safe. You don't owe me anything.*

I get it. Talk soon.

He's a smart guy and I know he wants to help, but I don't think *he* gets it. I can't just walk away from this.

Chapter
22

Bill's story appears around noon the next day on the *Sun-Sentinel*'s website. The headline reads: "Biker takeover feared as police probe hanging death."

The article draws heavily from biker and police sources; a few of them are identified but most are not. It begins:

> Local police and bikers alike are on edge with the arrival in town of members of the Popeyes, an international motorcycle gang with a history of high-level drug trafficking, extortion, arson, and murder.

That's old news to me but not to most people in our town, I suppose. The surprising part comes about halfway through the story:

> Certain members of the St. Thomas–based Annihilators Motorcycle Club and the Spartans,

based in London, met out of town recently to discuss a strategy for dealing with the Popeyes.

"The meeting was very hush-hush and was held in Guelph, an hour or so down the highway," a source close to events said. "It was apparently held there in an attempt to avoid detection by the Popeyes or members of the Annihilators and Spartans who are allied with the Popeyes or favor an alliance."

What's interesting about the meeting is that, according to Bill's sources, it took place at the time when Trent was killed. My brain kicks into overdrive. Anyone at the meeting has an alibi for the murder. Was Jamie there?

I keep reading:

Security was extremely tight for the Guelph meeting, as the local members of the Annihilators and Spartans are leery of betrayal from within their own ranks.

Meanwhile, police have ruled out suicide as the cause of Trent Wallace's death. While not a member of the Annihilators, Wallace was an associate of the club.

Wallace's body was found hanging from a beam of a club hangout where he was staying in St. Thomas.

His death was originally believed to be self-inflicted but is now under investigation by the police homicide unit. Police haven't yet commented about a suspect who has been taken into custody.

A picture's starting to come into focus. This supposed "secret meeting" happened during the time I lost contact with Jamie, and maybe it explains why Jamie has been so super-secretive. Talking about the meeting could get his friends killed by the Popeyes. It could get him killed too. While it seems crazy to say, a life sentence, in this case, would be better than what could happen on the streets. If you're not breathing, not much else matters.

Hopefully the story will push the police to investigate Trent's death more rigorously and also make the Popeyes feel like they're being watched. Maybe that's just wishful thinking, but I need something to hang on to.

Chapter
23

The article's nice but Jamie's still behind bars. There's a big difference between providing interesting reading and digging up enough evidence to set someone free.

I drive by the clubhouse minutes after reading the article, hoping I might bump into Ripper. I feel like he's one of the few people who could give me some advice about what I should be doing. I'm at loose ends, restless; I want to keep things moving and know I have to stay active so I don't get sucked into negative thinking.

But it's not Ripper I see when I pull up. It's Brenda, sitting on the porch on a cheap collapsible lawn chair, looking abandoned and drained. It's unusual to see women just hanging around outside the clubhouse alone, but I'm sure Brenda's not worried about appearances. I get out of the Cruze and walk over to her, finally catching her eye when I'm just a few feet away. We haven't seen each other or even spoken since Jamie's arrest.

"Hey."

Her voice sounds different. Vague, like she's talking to a stranger. Distant. And a bit sharp. I've never heard her like this before.

"Hey, I didn't expect to see you here," I say. I fidget with my keys, not quite sure what to do with my hands, or what to say next. "I'm a bit stressed," is what comes out.

She just stares. Not a warm stare.

"Why?" she asks after a moment or two of awkward silence.

"I feel like I'm doing what the cops should be doing—trying to prove that Jamie is innocent, I mean."

There. It's out. She barely acknowledges that I've spoken, just stares at me again. No cute bunny rabbit eyes today. That seems like so long ago. Her eyes are hard and focused and a bit angry.

When she finally speaks, it's not anything I want to hear. "Maybe they're just doing their job."

"Huh?"

I'm stalling, trying to figure out how to respond. This is what I was worried about—that she'd believe the worst, and hate me for it.

"Maybe they did their job." Her voice is soft but firm.

"Jamie didn't do it. I *know* he didn't."

A long pause.

"I hope you're right."

That's not exactly a vote of confidence. If it were anyone else, I'd be angry—and I admit I'm gutted by her words. But my emotions clearly aren't her top priority at the moment. And—and this is what I'm hanging on to—she stopped short of coming right out and saying he was guilty. I can work with that.

Brenda knows about club business, probably more than she realizes. She's hanging around the club-house, and between Trent and Carlito—no matter how squirmy thinking about her with him makes me feel—she's had access to more insider talk than I have. I can't afford to make her angry right now by defending Jamie. I have to take a different approach.

"I need your help," I finally say.

"Huh?" She looks at me like I'm out of my mind.

"I know you probably think I'm just sticking up for Jamie because he's my brother," I say, "but I really don't think . . ."

I'm desperate and I know it. It's painful to ask my next question.

"Can you ask around?"

Her answer is even more painful.

"I can ask Carlito. He's in the loop."

Is that a note of pride I hear in her voice? Will asking him for information mean flirting with him?

Who am I kidding? Bikers want more than flirtatious talk, and Brenda and Carlito already have a history.

How will Carlito react? Will he tell Brenda about his relationship with my mother? If so, will Brenda laugh at Mom? Or be disgusted by her? Or by me? Will Carlito act like I owe him a favor? Can this go any lower?

"You say you want the truth?" Brenda says.

Now I'm the one staring. Her face is so much colder and more severe than when I daydream about her.

"I think we're all capable . . . ," she begins. Then there's what feels like a long, long pause, though it probably only lasts a second or two. "Of anything," she finally finishes.

I must look surprised or hurt or both.

"Carlito's not perfect but maybe he can help," she says. "He's not all bad."

"He's . . ."

I'm struggling to finish my sentence. If she cares for me at all, she must know how deeply her words are cutting. Her face hardens, and she glares at me for a horrible second.

"He's not the one charged with killing Trent," she says.

I can't believe she just said that. Even she looks surprised. But it's out there now.

There's nothing left to say—nothing that I wouldn't regret forever. I get in my car and drive away.

Chapter
24

I lie on the couch at Jamie's house and try to calm down. I have the place to myself. It's too early to go home; seeing Mom will just make things worse.

My mind floats back to the spring after Dad moved out. I'm riding the school bus home and we pull up directly across the street from our house. I am carefully stepping off the bus when the other kids start to scream, "Fight! Fight!"

Through my fuzzy dream vision, I look out toward our house and see a man charging up our driveway with a big knife in his right hand. Another man is running away. He crashes through the hedge and disappears. They both look like giants to me, but anyone who was angry and holding a knife would have seemed ten feet tall back then. They are both older than my brother, too, in their midtwenties at least. One has long, wild, scraggly hair, the other a shaved head and a goatee. I have never seen either of them before.

Next I see Jamie on the front walkway, his fists clenched. He's the age I am now—seventeen.

What follows is like some crazy slow-motion scene from an action movie: first, the goateed stranger hoists the knife over his head and aims it down at my brother. There's a collective gasp from the kids on the school bus. A few turn their heads away so they don't have to see blood.

I stand in stunned silence on the steps of the bus as Jamie glides to his left, toward the knife, and raises a forearm to protect his head. He doesn't look at all scared or even surprised. It's as if he's been waiting all of his life for this.

I feel like I'm watching some movie-screen commando, not my big brother. His right leg sweeps up and his shin connects hard with the man's right inner thigh, freezing him where he stands. A slight pivot and then Jamie delivers two more blows directly into his groin, with the studied arc of a punter sending a football high into the air. The man crumples to the ground like he's melting. I am too far away to hear much but I can imagine his groaning.

The kids on the bus, especially the boys, let out a collective moan. On the playground, we call striking the groin "bagging someone," and no one ever finds it funny when it happens to him. As we watch the real, adult version, I can feel some of my classmates' eyes shift toward me in a combination of fear, disgust, and awe.

Jamie scoops the man up by the underarms and drags him into the garage, oblivious to our stares. I'm off the bus now, standing alone under a tree across the street, and can only gawk as Jamie backs out in the family car and drives away. I can't see the guy, but I guess he's in the car somewhere. I've wondered about that more than once in the years since, but I've never asked Jamie about it.

Over the next few hours, I keep expecting the cops to arrive at our door but they never do. The next I see of Jamie is later that day, when he praises my mother for the roast chicken she's made for dinner, insisting it's as good as a meal at Swiss Chalet, the local restaurant where, he tells us, he took his first date years ago. As dinner conservation goes, it's painfully normal, even dull, and all I can do is watch him in amazement. I love Jamie, but for the first time I realize there are parts of his life he cannot or will not ever share with me.

After that day, the rough kids at school seem to warm up to me and the straight-arrow kids give me a wide berth. Fear and respect aren't the same thing, but they are at least close cousins. Soon, Jamie announces he is moving out on his own.

Years later, my brother was my biggest and loudest fan during school football games. I loved seeing the look of pride on his face when I ran out onto the field and hearing him cheer when I made a tackle. We've talked a lot about football over the years, but never about that man with the knife in our front yard. We've talked about girls too, usually at Jamie's instigation.

Once he told me, "The best advice I can give you is this: don't fall in love with a girl who can't generate her own self-esteem."

"Huh?" I remember replying. I think I was twelve at the time.

"You need someone who already feels good about herself. If she needs you to make her feel happy and you're not around, she'll go looking for someone else to do the job."

It didn't mean much at the time, but I can see now that he thought these were some seriously wise words.

When I think back to those days and months after Dad left, the smell of beer and stale wine and tobacco comes rushing back. So does the memory of Mom with glassy red, vacant eyes. I had never felt embarrassed about her before, but that's when things started to change.

It was Jamie who picked up the slack, making my lunch for school and teaching me how to ride a bike and stressing the importance of eating carrots and spinach and not just potato chips. In time, his fight with the man with the knife on our lawn became like something out of a dream, or a particularly scary bedtime story.

I have always believed that I know the real Jamie. The real Jamie tucked me into bed and didn't tease me if I cried at night because I still missed Dad sometimes. The real Jamie defended people. He didn't attack them.

The real Jamie also often wandered away and got lost. Now it's my job to bring him back.

Chapter
25

Maybe I'll crash here at Jamie's for a few days. The image of Carlito lounging around in our living room is stuck in my mind; the last thing I need is a repeat performance, or a scene with Mom.

The idea comes to me late that night, when I'm on the verge of nodding off. Wherever I'm crashing, one thing is for sure: it's time to have a serious talk with Ripper. For all of his hippy-dippy Zen master talk, Ripper can be surprisingly practical and clear-headed when the situation calls for it—and this situation calls for it. Jamie will be back in court again soon and we need a lawyer. That means I need Ripper to get the club to help with the legal bills. I don't want to beg but I'm feeling desperate. If all else fails, I'll stay home with Mom next year and work at whatever job I can get, but I know this will mean saying good-bye to my football dreams. Jamie might get a life sentence behind bars. I might get one in this town.

Traffic is pretty light the next morning as I drive to Ripper's place, which sits next to an auto body shop a couple of blocks from the clubhouse. I imagine he'll make time to talk with me, but I know there's plenty he won't tell me. For example, the meeting in Guelph. I'm sure Ripper knew all about it, maybe even attended or planned it, but I'm not going to hear about it from him. He probably also won't tell me anything about why Jamie was arguing with Trent that night, although I'm sure he knows something about the bad blood between them. And I don't think I can ask him about which members of the Annihilators want to patch over to the Popeyes and which ones are actively resisting an alliance. My guess is that Ripper's supporters are all resisters and Trollop's supporters would love the power of a Popeyes patch.

As I drive, I think of how furious Trollop must have been to see the photo of Ripper at Trent's funeral in the *Sun-Sentinel*, after he'd discouraged the Annihilators from going. Trollop doesn't seem to get that he's no longer president; Ripper just humors him, but in Trollop's mind, at least, there's a power struggle going on between them.

A connection with the Popeyes could be lucrative in terms of potential meth-trade profits, and Trollop likely sees Ripper as getting in the way of that. As Bill explained, nearby London's a big fat market just waiting to be tapped. But Ripper's almost prudish about drugs. He doesn't like anything used to excess; he told me once that he didn't trust anything that doesn't grow in the ground.

Ripper lives in a small, detached two-and-a-half-story brick house with a garage that he added on one side. It's not posh, by any stretch, but it is cozy in its own way. When I pull up, Ripper is on the front lawn, looking grubby and holding a shovel.

"What's up?" I say.

"Moving Jimmy Hoffa."

He's referring to the old Teamsters boss who went missing under mysterious circumstances back in the 1960s. A lot of Ripper's jokes assume you're at least fifty years old.

His neighborhood is in the midst of a slow gentrification, though things are moving particularly slowly on Ripper's street. There are Volvos and Subarus in the driveways now, although you don't have to look too far to see rusted-out vehicles on front lawns and uncut grass. And at Ripper's place, it's like the calendar stopped sometime back in the 1960s.

"I was hoping to pick your brain a bit," I say. I may feel desperate but I'm at least trying to be cool.

"If you can find it, you can pick it."

"I've got a bunch of things I'd like to ask you."

"Such as?"

I really need to ask about a lawyer for Jamie, but I decide to ease toward that. "What's the problem between you and Trollop about?"

Normally, this might be too forward, but these aren't normal times.

"So many things. One example: once he and a couple of his buddies showed up at the London Pride Parade waving Confederate flags."

Ripper maintains a poker face but his eyes seem to roll for a second. I stifle a sigh. So this is how it's going to be? I'm going to have to wade through all of the nutty stuff before I get anything real? Fine, I can play this game.

"When?"

"Ten years ago or so."

I would have been in grade two. Jamie wasn't in the club yet. No wonder I've never heard about it.

"What was his point?"

"He doesn't need a point."

"Huh?"

"His point is that he needs attention. That's generally the way things start and end with him."

Now we're getting somewhere. Ripper's opening up. I need to keep him talking.

"So what happened?"

"Me and a couple of other guys really called him out on it. Thought we were going to fight it out right in the clubhouse."

"You were really that mad?"

"I was furious. We're a nonconformist lifestyle. Outsiders. We're supposed to be cool about things, not jerks."

It's kind of funny to think about Jamie's biker friends as committed social dissidents, but Ripper is deadly serious.

"I told him the people marching in that parade had more parts than he does," he says next. He smiles at that memory and then continues. "That was what really got him. Plus, he did it wearing club colors. He dragged all of us into his stupid drama. Made us all look like idiots. There's a reason we don't talk a lot publicly."

"To keep the police guessing?"

He just rolls his eyes, like a wise, cranky uncle. "Sure. But also to keep a certain image. If you keep your mouth shut, people might at least think you have something smart to say. If you're screaming like an idiot at a parade, waving a flag that has come to be associated with racism, it's public knowledge you're a moron. Especially if you wind up in the paper like he did. Better to keep some mystery. Things were never the same after that between me and Trollop."

"I get it."

"Can you *really* get me something?"

"Sure."

"I'm dying for a coffee."

He's joking, but not really.

He's sitting on the front porch steps now, looking his age for a change. The digging can wait.

"Not a problem. Why don't I run over to Starbucks? I could use a jolt myself." I'm more relaxed now. "What kind?"

"Make it a venti Americano."

He smirks a little. I'm a little surprised that Ripper is familiar with Starbucks jargon, but then again, nothing shocks me about bikers anymore.

"I'll be back in twenty minutes."

"You know where to find me."

It takes a little longer than I expected at Starbucks. The person in front of me has trouble deciding which whipped cream drizzle drink he wants, and then the app on his phone won't work when it's time to pay. At this pace, Ripper's going to think I forgot all about him.

On the drive back, a dark green Ford truck headed toward me swerves crazily into and then out of my lane when I round a corner a couple of blocks from Ripper's house. It races by me and I get a look at the driver, who appears to be having a panic attack. The guy in the passenger seat has his head ducked down and his face is obscured by both a cap and a hoodie. Good thing I put lids on these coffees or I'd have an $11 mess on the front seat of my car.

A block from the house, an ambulance rips past me, sirens blaring.

I instantly tense up.

I arrive at Ripper's to see a cop putting yellow crime-scene tape around the porch where Ripper and I were talking not half an hour ago. There's blood all over the steps. So much blood. I take a gulp of air and fight the urge to toss my cookies. I'm not normally a queasy guy, but I know whose blood this is. Until this moment, Ripper has always seemed untouchable to me. He just seemed too tough, too smart, too respected to be vulnerable to anything. But now he's nowhere to be seen.

I pull up behind one of several police cars stopped outside the house. I feel numb.

"What happened?" I ask without getting out of the car.

"Shooting. You know who lives here?"

"No." I feel a bit dirty about the lie but I'm stuck in it now. "Are they going to be okay?"

"He was breathing when he left," the cop says. I give my head a little shake, as if I'm just appalled at what's happening in my neighborhood, and slowly drive away. I glance in my rearview mirror to see another cop taping off the patch of garden where Ripper was weeding.

I'm not sure why I sidestepped the cops. It was a reflex more than a conscious decision. Ripper isn't one to talk much with the police, so I don't feel I'm doing him any disrespect. I don't think anything really. I just drive.

Chapter
26

I feel just like I did when I was a little kid on the verge of a panic attack. My breathing's almost out of control, and I'm finding it hard to focus. My brain is ricocheting from one thought to the next, rapid-fire. I need to slow it down. Get a grip. I could easily have been at Ripper's house when the shooting happened. That could be my blood all over his front steps. The gunman was probably in that green truck. I wish I'd seen its occupants' faces more clearly.

A number of police cars are parked outside the emergency ward when I arrive at the hospital. I try to walk in casually so that no one will look twice at me, but I'm jerky and tense. There are uniforms stationed by the entrance and beside the elevators, too, clearly on alert. I'm feeling freaked at the sight of all of this security when I spot Ripper's daughter, Frances, across the lobby.

I don't know Ripper's wife at all, but I do know a thing or two about Frances. She will never, ever be mistaken for a biker chick. She looks like a school-teacher or a nurse, someone who has a sensible, caring job. She's not plain but she's certainly not going out of her way to attract attention. I've heard she lives in town and works in a Home Depot and is married to a nice guy who designs webpages and drives a mini-van. I've seen her around here and there, but never, obviously, at any of Trollop's parties.

"I'm really sorry," I say.

"Thanks."

Her voice is flat but she seems sincere.

"Any word?"

"Not yet. A nurse said it'll be a while."

I see a cop looking at me. He doesn't avert his gaze when he notices me noticing him.

"I was with him, right before . . ."

"Did you see anything?"

"No. Well, I saw a truck driving away, but that's it."

She's staring into space. I'm not sure where she stands on the biker code and cooperating, or not, with the police.

"I'm sorry about your brother," she says, suddenly present again.

"Yeah, sucks. He didn't . . . I went to see your dad because I was hoping the club might help out with a lawyer."

I feel antsy with all the police around. It's like they're all looking at me, listening to me.

"Do you need anything?" I ask, knowing it sounds lame.

"I'm not sending you for coffee," she says. She pauses for a second and then smiles. She's got her dad's sense of humor.

"Oh. You heard that." I smile too, not just at the joke but at what it tells me. If Frances knows I went out for coffee, it means Ripper's awake and talking.

She smirks, then her face turns serious again.

"Do you think the club's under attack?" I ask.

She shrugs her shoulders.

"Who knows? But if Dad stays out of commission, Trollop will officially become president of the Annihilators again. Lord help us."

"Sometimes I think of your dad as my cool old uncle," I tell Frances, and her eyes sparkle.

"What about Trollop?" she counters.

I don't want to call him a psycho and I don't want to lie. I let my pained facial expression do the talking for me. Trollop as acting president is a scary thought. He could push the club toward the Popeyes or he could hook up with the Spartans to block the Popeyes from moving in. From the way he was sucking up to the scary Nomad in the red vest at the barn party, I have little doubt what he would like to do.

"The president also has control of the emergency fund," Frances adds.

My heart sinks. That fund would be the source of lawyer money for Jamie. I'd rather not have to turn to the likes of Trollop for help but I may not have a choice. The worst part of the biker life, as I see it, is having to trust your fate to idiots like him.

"You working with Bill Taylor now?" she asks me next.

I'm surprised she knows him. "Yeah, I'm at the *Sun-Sentinel*. He's way senior."

She's studying my face.

"You know him?" I ask.

"He used to live around here. He and my Dad were buddies, back in a different life." There's a long pause, and then, "They still stay in touch."

There's a faraway look in her eyes.

"What's your number?" she adds. "I'll let you know if there's any update."

We exchange information and I walk toward the door. I have the feeling that every cop in the place has his or her eyes on me as I climb into my car and turn the key.

Chapter
27

As nauseating as the idea is, it's time to go see Trollop. Ripper can't help me right now and I'm running out of time. I remember something Bill once told me about how his best sources aren't usually found in the front pews of a church. I guess I'm in the same boat. I need money for a lawyer; I don't need to love the guy.

Trollop runs his courier business from an office about twenty minutes away from the hospital. It's in a nondescript strip mall, between a pet-supplies store and a kitchen renovation center.

I'm calmer now, and feel like I've slipped back into the Zone. I'm able to slow down and focus on my breathing and on the task at hand. Besides the lawyer, I need to keep on trying to learn more about who really killed Trent. His death must be connected to the attack on Ripper. Right?

Trollop's hunched over his desk when I walk into his office. He's face down in paperwork, and for a few seconds, he doesn't even notice I'm there.

There is nothing in the office that hints at Trollop's biker identity. No family photos either. On his desk is a small, rounded object that looks like a seashell, except that it's bony. Something looks wrong about it. Could it be human? I'm sure he would tell me if I asked, but I don't feel like asking today.

Trollop flinches when he sees me.

"You startled me," he says.

The man's paranoid on a good day, and I imagine he's nervous now. I'm guessing he knows that Ripper's just been shot—news travels fast in this world—and maybe Trollop's worried someone's coming after him too. I can't help but think of a joke Ripper once told me: "Help, I'm being chased by paranoids."

There are two cell phones sitting at opposite ends of the desk. My mind goes back to the barbecue and Trollop posing for a selfie with the big Popeye in the Kevlar vest, like some biker fanboy. Not for the first time, it occurs to me that it could be important to learn more about that guy. When he came to town, people started acting differently, and not in a good way.

Trollop looks up and adjusts his glasses. "Yo, bro. So sad about your brother. What can I do you for?"

I try not to wince. In his mind, it's a cool and original line. It's like he aspires to be a cartoon character.

"It's pretty screwed up. I'm really worried about Jamie."

"We all are."

He says "we" as if he's a central player in this. He's not the one potentially facing a life in prison, or the one who might lose a real brother. Still, he scrunches up his face in a semblance of deep concern.

"They might not have much on Jamie, bro," he says. "Don't panic. Be solid. We'll get through this."

Much on him? How can they have *anything* on him? He's suggesting my brother is guilty. And what does he mean by "be solid"? Is he reminding me not to be a rat?

"I can't believe what happened to Ripper," I say, watching his face. "I just came from the hospital."

"I know. Unreal," he says.

After a pause, he continues in a tone that seems a little too bright. "You know, I have a buddy who could say he and Jamie were together when the murder happened."

The idea immediately offends me. Maybe because I don't want us to be indebted to Trollop. Maybe because we shouldn't have to lie to prove Jamie's not a killer. And—most important—maybe lying will just dig Jamie in deeper.

"That's okay," I say slowly.

Then Trollop startles me. "See you're friendly with the cook's sister," he says next.

When did he notice? Am I that obvious? Is he that observant?

I don't say anything.

"Best not to sell out your brother for a woman, no matter how sweet she is," he tells me, smirking.

The way he says "sweet" makes me feel like punching him.

I could have him whimpering on the floor in seconds but I hold back. For her sake. For my brother's sake. Still, I would love to. I can see how someone could turn violent in this environment. I take a deep breath instead. Stay in the Zone.

There's a knock on the door and a dispatcher tells Trollop that one of his trucks has been illegally parked and is about to be towed.

Trollop swears and jumps up from his chair. "Be right back."

The next couple of minutes feel like the middle of a big football game, when there's no time to think, only to react. No time for paralysis by analysis, as my coaches would say. I scoop up one of the phones from Trollop's desk, tap a couple of buttons, and start searching for photos.

Nothing.

I pick up the other phone, still trying desperately not to panic. I find a folder of photos and start scrolling down.

Jackpot!

I'm looking at a picture of Trollop and the Popeye in the red vest. Trollop's grinning. The other biker is grimacing.

I send a copy to myself, erase the "sent" file, then slide the phone back down on his desk. If I can learn more about the guy in the photo maybe I'll be able to start puzzling out the truth about Trent's murder—and Jamie's role in it.

I panic for a moment, remembering that Trollop is just the type of clown who'd have a surveillance camera hidden in his office. I can only hope that isn't the case. Too late to do anything about it anyway.

Before I know it, Trollop is back. My heart's pumping so hard I'm surprised he can't hear it from across the room. It's time to get out of here. Forget about asking for legal help for Jamie—I'm barely keeping it together.

"How's the knee?" he asks as I'm leaving. Everyone seems to want to hear about this. Don't they know there are more important things going on?

"Good thanks. I'm back in the gym. Going there right now, in fact."

Moments later, I'm in my car in the parking lot. I have to make it past a parking attendant and a barrier gate before I'm home free. As I'm starting the car, I forward Trollop's photo to Bill Taylor.

You know this guy with Trollop? I text. *He could be worth checking out.*

Then I'm out the gate. If Trollop has a hidden camera, he hasn't checked it yet.

When I'm a couple of blocks down the street, I pull over to catch my breath and see that I have a new text message from Ripper. The fact that he can text me at all is a relief, since it must mean he's doing okay back at the hospital. The message reads: *Club can cover $5,000 for lawyer's retainer. Afraid we can't handle more but it's a start. Good luck.*

It's not much but it's something. As things stand right now, all we have is enough money for one roll of the dice . . .

Chapter
28

My next stop is the gym. It's the best place I know to clear my head and focus my thoughts. It's after suppertime and the place is almost empty; I have the bench press area all to myself. I really need a hard workout today, and not just to make up for the ones I've missed over the past week.

My plan is to deliberately load the bar with more weight than I can handle and press until my arms and chest feel like jelly. It's a great way to safely stress the muscles so they rebuild aggressively and you come back even stronger.

There's a new guy in the gym today. His head is shaved and he's sporting a soul patch. He has about twenty pounds on me and looks like he knows his way around a weight room. I don't know him but I need a spotter and this isn't rocket science.

He seems friendly enough and agrees to help when

I ask. It'll only take five minutes but some guys are really uptight about their routines, with their timers and exercise logs and protein shakes and little bags of supplements. They don't want you looking in their direction, let alone asking them for help.

All I need the spotter to do is keep the weight from coming down hard on me as I near the end of my final three lifts. By then, I'll be seeing stars on a purple background but I don't want him to make it too easy. A good spotter can do the job with just two fingers touching the bar.

He stands behind my head, out of sight but ready to help, as I lie down on the bench and grip the barbell.

First . . . the weight goes up without too much trouble.

Second . . . I exhale and my elbows lock. I see a little flash of purple but I'm okay.

I pause for maybe a second before I lower the bar again. Slowly. My arms are shaking a little under the weight.

I repeat the process a second time and it's not too much worse. More purple flashes. More shaking of my arms. But it's doable.

The third rep is where it can change fast. I take pains not to bounce the barbell off of my chest; there's enough weight here to do some serious damage. I barely get it off my chest when everything seizes up.

Now the stars are everywhere, and up close. That's my signal that I'm maxed out. I'm going to need help.

I let the bar rest on my torso. I see a burst of purple stars. Then black. Then yellow. Like my own personal fireworks show.

Nothing's happening. I can't move the weight. Where's the spotter?

I nod my head to signal that it's time for him to step in.

Nothing.

Another nod.

Still nothing.

Perhaps he's trying to respect my wishes to make the lift hard. But can't he tell I need help?

Another second passes.

And another.

White exploding lights.

No help.

I'm alone here.

I can't move the bar at all to release the pressure, and I'm feeling faint.

He must know there's a problem.

He must know this is dangerous.

He must know I could die.

I nod my head frantically. The weight is impossible for me to manage now. I'm not strong enough to keep it from crushing my chest if my arms give out.

Everything has gone black, and I'm seeing bursts of stars, one after another.

I'm about to pass out.

I look up at my spotter.

He's no more than a shadow but he's still there. I can't see him but I can hear his breathing. He's just standing there, motionless and silent.

If the bar slides up, just a little, it could snap my neck or strangle me. If it slides down, just a little, it could crush my ribs. I don't have enough air in my lungs to curse him or beg him for help or scream in distress, not that there's anyone else around anyway.

I could die here and it would look like an accident. People would think I was just being careless trying to lift a heavy weight without a spotter.

I hear a hoarse whisper. Something about minding my own business.

Then, "Back off." That's what it sounds like anyway. I'm physically unable to reply, even if I wanted to.

The bar is rising now. Slowly. He's barely helping.

I feel like I'm going to faint, but I struggle to keep the heavy weight moving.

Finally, there's a clank as the barbell lands back on the rack. I'm too drained to move. My arms and chest muscles are shot.

I open my eyes, breathing deeply and doing my best to wrap my head around what's just happened here. Did I imagine the whole thing? Is the lack of sleep over the past few days finally catching up with me? Or was I just threatened—warned to back off of trying to sort out what really happened between Trent and Jamie? That possibility sends new thoughts flying around my brain—angry thoughts, *furious* thoughts. This is one of my favorite places in the world, somewhere I never thought I could be in danger. Finally, I sit up and look around. My spotter is nowhere to be seen.

Chapter
29

I dream about the police again. It's fuzzy and confused but I wake up in the middle of the night a couple of times with my head full of frantic sounds and upsetting images of uniforms and cars and guns.

Checking my email, I see that Bill has sent me a bunch of stories in French and English about the guy in Trollop's selfie. The first article I pick up begins dramatically:

> George Baker—aka "Baker the Undertaker,"
> a member of the high-ranking Nomads unit
> within the Montreal motorcycle club known as
> the Popeyes—walked away from double murder
> charges today after a key witness surprised
> prosecutors by abruptly changing his testimony
> in court. Baker declined to comment as he left
> the courthouse.

The rest of the stories are similarly ominous. Baker's name pops up in several reports about drug trafficking and murder, and I'm treated to his terrifying mug shot in a couple of them. Most of the incidents the articles describe took place in the Montreal area, but his alleged misdeeds have spread to Toronto and even Vancouver over the years. Witnesses seem to suffer memory loss or go away whenever Baker the Undertaker gets into trouble.

You really want to get this guy pissed at you? Bill asks in his message.

The media pieces and court reports confirm that the Popeyes are connected to serious mob people in Montreal and Toronto, as well as the Colombian and Mexican drug cartels and several Jamaican and Haitian street gangs. No wonder everyone in my brother's world seems afraid of them.

Bill has also sent some material about law enforcement's use of encryption breaking and something called Stingray surveillance in investigating both the Mafia and outlaw bikers. One story in a national newspaper reads:

Police are fighting to keep a lid on the release of spy technology that they've begun using to tap into cellular phones as part of the fight against organized crime and motorcycle gangs.

Documents filed in the Ontario Court of Appeal show that federal government lawyers

have acknowledged the police's use of a spy tool
known as a "mobile device identifier."

In policing circles, it's more commonly called
a "Stingray" and it's capable of collecting phone
and text conversations that take place within a
kilometer of affiliated portable towers.

Government lawyers are fighting hard to keep
further details under wraps leading up to a hearing scheduled for next month in Toronto.

Paul Bates, a researcher with the Citizen Lab
at the University of Toronto's Munk School of
Global Affairs, said the devices have been used
in the past but that this marks "the first time
authorities have been caught out in court."

"This has profound implications for law
enforcement, the cellular phone industry, and
the privacy concerns of law-abiding citizens,"
Bates said.

Another story notes that even encrypted cellular
devices aren't immune from Stingray surveillance:

"What if the police knew how to tap into not
just everyone's phones, but their encrypted messages as well?" one journalist has asked. "That's
essentially what's going on now with the Royal
Canadian Mounted Police in Canada, which has
the power to decrypt at will messages intercepted
in a massive, ongoing organized-crime probe."

I have to wonder: Were there Stingrays in the Guelph area when the Annihilators and Spartans were holding their secret meeting?

Plenty of local bikers are opposed to the Popeyes pushing into their area, Bill has added in his message. *The guys who went to the Guelph meeting are taking a huge gamble. They're risking a bullet from their own clubs as well as the Popeyes. They have to pray no one sells them out.*

Really appreciate it, I reply. *But I need a plan. I'll go nuts if I just sit here.*

Here's an idea, he writes next. *Some of the Popeyes are big fans of Frank Lupo Jr, a boxer related to an old mob boss. He's not a great fighter, but he's game and it gives them a chance to show their support for the mob and have a little fun as well. His ring nickname is "Hitman."* Seriously.

I see from one of the links Bill has sent that Frank Jr. has a bout in Mississauga this weekend. It would be interesting to see how the various members of the Spartans and Annihilators are treated by the Popeyes in that setting.

I should go, I type.

If you do, please be careful.

It's something—a lead, Bill might say—but I still feel hopeless. What have I really learned? I already knew meth paid big money. Big deal if I have some media reports about that. I already knew Baker was a serious bad guy. So what if I have his name now? The Stingray stuff is sort of interesting, but I don't really know what to make of it. I have to keep moving, but I have the sinking feeling that I'm just running around in circles.

Chapter
30

The boxing event is taking place in a recently built hockey complex off Highway 403, an hour or so from St. Thomas. I park at the back of the lot, far away from the crowded area near the arena entrance. The last thing I need is to scratch or box in some gangster's Escalade. Fancy oversized vehicles are everywhere, and mostly black. You never see those guys in a lime-green Smart car or a Prius. The high-end car show around me makes my Cruze stick out like a Vespa at a biker field day.

This parking lot was the site of an alleged mob hit about four months ago. It took place after another boxing night. Someone shot a Toronto restaurateur and his bodyguard at close range while they were seated in their BMW. This was a big-time crime, and I only know about it through the news. As I remember, both of the victims were carrying handguns, but neither of them managed to draw. Things must have seemed okay—right until the moment they saw the assassin's gun pointed at them, I guess.

The old disco hit "Stayin' Alive" blares over the loudspeakers as I take my place in the cheap seats. VIP seats down by the ring are $150 each, triple what I paid. I tell myself it's probably better to be hidden up here anyway: plus, $50 isn't exactly peanuts, especially since I no longer have a paycheck coming in. My seat gives me a clear view of the VIP section, where the Popeyes are gathered.

I can see Baker the Undertaker down there with three or four others who look like bikers too. No one's wearing gang colors. They're forbidden in the arena, but Baker and his buddies still have that big-club look. Mixed in with them are some intimidating guys who look too slick to be bikers, dressed in a rich-dude-casual style: sports jackets, expensive jeans, and fitted T-shirts. It's a safe bet these are some of the mobsters Bill said would be here.

Then a more familiar face comes into view: Carlito strolls up to one of the ringside tables to say hello. The bikers and their fancy friends give him some time, but they don't offer him a seat. He seems happy enough with the attention he gets, and returns to a seat a few rows back from the ring.

I text Brenda.

At a boxing match. Checking things out.

We've had no contact since our tense encounter at the clubhouse, and I have no idea what kind of response to expect. But I want her to know that I'm working on this, that I'm still trying to prove that Jamie had nothing to do with her brother's murder.

No reply.

Five minutes go by.

Still no reply.

Rejection? She's still mad? She has something better to do? She's with someone? All of the above? There's nothing I can do but wait.

The first matchup features a guy named McTavish, who's led out by guys in kilts playing the bagpipes and a drum. He's pasty-white and lean as a whip and doesn't look like much, but he devours a heavily muscled black fighter from Montreal. Several members of the crowd whoop appreciatively as the referee stops the fight in the second round with blood pouring from the Montrealer's face.

The next three bouts are all variations on the same theme. Fit, sinewy, borderline-skinny Ontario fighters outbox burlier, less skilled plodders from out of the area. Seeing local boys beat up on the visitors goes over well with the audience, who hoot and shout their approval.

Finally, it's the Hitman's turn.

Frank Jr. enters the ring with the Rolling Stones' "Start Me Up" on the speakers. The fight announcer clearly enjoys shouting out "the Hitman!" in the introductions, in case anyone has forgotten the box-er's family background. Frank Jr. is wearing a serious scowl and has an average body for a boxer, while his local opponent is rangy and loose-limbed, with a pale complexion and a shock of red hair.

Immediately after the opening bell, Frank Jr. rushes the taller fighter, hungry for a quick knockout. His opponent sidesteps him easily and connects with a jab to the side of the head as Frank Jr. lurches past.

"Hit the Hitman," someone shouts as Frank Jr. absorbs a faceful of leather.

They say that every fighter has a plan until he is hit. Frank Jr.'s plan was clearly to take out his op-ponent early, before his own lack of skills and limited punching power were exposed. That plan is derailed quickly.

Through the first several rounds, Frank Jr. keeps swinging and missing. There's something almost noble in the fact that he won't just go down or stop trying. Another *pop-pop-pop* and Frank Jr.'s legs buckle. The bell rings to end the round.

When it sounds again for the start of the sixth round, Frank Jr. wearily pulls himself up off his stool. His trainer takes a hard look into his fighter's eyes, gives him a fatherly hug, then turns to the referee and waves his arms back and forth.

Mercifully, the fight is over.

Frank Jr. staggers over to the victor and embraces him before being led off to the medical room.

Back at the mobsters' table, they don't seem to particularly care that their man just got pummeled, and the bikers seem equally indifferent. Baker the Undertaker barely glances toward the ring as he stands and gets ready to leave.

And that's it. The fights are done. I head back to the car with a familiar knot forming in my stomach. This intelligence-gathering expedition feels like a waste of $50, not to mention gas money. I don't know what I expected to find here, but whatever it was, I came up short.

Chapter
31

A black Dodge truck pulls out from the spot next to me as I text Brenda from the parking lot: *Just leaving. The big guy from Popeyes is obviously close to some mob guys.*

It's no great scoop, but it's a nice excuse to try again to make contact with her.

You okay? she texts back.

That was quick. And she's concerned.

For sure. In parking lot now. Tried to text you before. Battery weak. Had to recharge. I need a new one.

I guess her earlier silence wasn't a rejection after all. That's something. And the tension from our talk outside the clubhouse seems to have passed, or at least lessened. There's a lot going on in the parking lot now. Everyone is trying to leave and no one is directing traffic. There are some pretty high-end BMWs, Porsches, and Mercedes in this jumble, as well as a smattering of Audis and even a few Maseratis. Their drivers aren't eager to scratch their cars or bump anyone, so aggressive drivers in the big muscle trucks like Ford F-150s and Chevy Silverados get a pretty wide berth.

We're all trapped in our vehicles now. It would be easy to walk up to any car and fire a few shots and not be noticed until it was too late. When did I start thinking like this?

Are you okay? I text.

Bit blue, sorry.

Don't be sorry. You had a week from hell.

Don't believe in hell, but yeah.

Well I believe in heaven, I write.

Really?

I believe in something, I reply. *Hard to define.*

Hopefully that ends this line of discussion. Life on Earth is confusing enough without getting into the big questions of what comes next. I'm stuck in the back of the parking lot for now so I have time to text, but I'm not really in a deep-thoughts mood. She clearly is.

I think we're basically alone, she writes. *People make up things so they don't have to feel lonely.*

You aren't alone, I offer.

You are a very sweet boy.

I'm not so sure what to make of the words "sweet" or "boy."

I doubt she calls Carlito a boy, and I definitely don't want to be treated like her little brother. She's special, and I want her to realize I'm a guy, not just some generic nice person. If we were living three hundred years ago, I'd cross the ocean, make my fortune, then return in triumph to win her heart. All I can do right now is text her using both thumbs.

Are you outside? I ask.

Yeah.

Do you see a big star up there?

Yeah. Actually, I see a lot of them.

Okay. See the moon? I'm looking at it too, I type. *We're doing the same thing. So we're together.*

Oh God. Did I just type that? I have seen kids teased unmercifully for this sort of thing. This might be a good time for a mobster to walk up to the Cruze and put a slug or two in me. I could load and aim the gun for him.

Thank you, she texts.

So she thinks my tone is okay. I decide to ride the mood further.

The moon changes every day, I type, *but it never goes away.*

We both pause, and not just to give our thumbs a break. I'm pretty sure she has never had a moment like this with Carlito.

A minute later she continues: *What about when the moon isn't out?*

It's 10:20 now, I text. *Twice a day, at 10:20, you think of me and I'll think of you.*

That's very sweet, she replies. *I will.*

"Sweet" again. I'm wondering whether to keep going or just bask in the afterglow of this exchange. It's much easier to communicate with her when I'm not spellbound by her eyes.

Then she adds: *You really believe in a God?*

Yup, but my heaven has a wing for nice honest atheists.

Lol, she replies. *Thought your heaven was the gym. Or the football field.*

At least she knows I'm an athlete, so I guess I've got a little masculine cred with her. *That stuff's dumb in the big scheme of things,* I write. *Running around with a little ball. Who cares really when you get down to it?* It's how I feel, to be honest. She could convince me to quit sports and the gym in a second.

No it's not. You love it.

Think of how great you are, I type. I have totally lost any filter I ever had. It's like driving fast at night without brakes.

Night, she types.

A few seconds later, just as I'm signing off, she adds, *XO.*

Chapter
32

The morning after the fights I drive to the jail as soon as I get up. Today, Jamie walks into the visiting room as stiffly as an old man. His lower lip is purple and at least twice its normal size. There's a jagged black line below his mouth from stitches. And his left eye is so bruised and puffy the outline of his cheekbone isn't visible.

"You okay?"

It's a stupid question and his answer isn't any better: "Fine."

I try not to stare at his face. There's no point asking what happened. He wouldn't answer me and he'd just be annoyed. He needs to maintain some pride, and it's unlikely becoming known as a squealer would help his jailhouse reputation.

I doubt the Popeyes are behind his injuries. I'm sure they have contacts on the inside and could have gotten to him, but if they really wanted to hurt him, they would have done a better job. He'd be in the hospital, maybe the morgue. I suspect there doesn't have to be a great reason for attacking someone in jail so I decide to let it go.

It's not long before I can sense that Jamie regrets coming out to see me. He's not as talkative as usual, and he fidgets with his hands the way he did when his stuttering was really a problem. I also doubt I'm going to learn anything new from him today. I feel like things are getting worse, that we're sinking lower and lower.

But there is something positive to report. "I managed to get $5,000 from the club for a lawyer's retainer," I say. "It's not much, but we can at least hire someone good. We have to make it count."

Jamie looks confused. I expected him to be happy and grateful—a good defense could save his bacon and I made it happen! There's clearly something he doesn't want to share with me. I guess a lawyer would demand that he tell the truth about what he knows about Trent's death. Does he have an alibi he's not telling me or the police about? And would he tell a lawyer? He would have to cooperate with his defense counsel, wouldn't he?

I'm still infuriated that he's staying quiet. I can't imagine he's feeling good about his future. How will he cope if he has to spend the next twenty-five years in prison? More than anyone I know, Jamie needs his own space. At his house, he gets agitated if anyone even touches his special coffee blend or the TV remote.

"Were you at a meeting with some guys from the Spartans the night Trent died?" I ask. "It's really important that I know."

For a moment, he looks startled, but quickly regains his composure. I'd take his expression as a "yes," but I need more. I feel like I might have just said something very dangerous, that maybe we should be whispering. And I know that our conversation is probably being recorded, but at this point I don't care. I need the truth to start coming out.

"Seriously, this really matters," I insist. "Were you there?"

Right now, I wouldn't be surprised if he got up and walked back to his cell instead of answering me.

Instead, he gives me the slightest of nods.

A door swings open and it's time for us to go our separate ways. This time, Jamie doesn't order me to stop digging into what happened to Trent. He knows he can't stop me anyway, but maybe it's more than that.

The clock is ticking.

Maybe I can finally show he's not the killer, without betraying anyone's trust or getting anyone else killed.

"Don't tell Mom about my accident," he says.

His voice sounds funny as he says the word "accident." I say nothing.

"I'm serious. Don't tell Mom."

It's an order and he expects me to obey.

I nod.

"Thanks," he says as the guards lead him away.

◄○►

Mom is coming in to see Jamie just as I'm leaving. She got a ride from a friend or took a cab, I suppose. I also suppose I'll wait and drive her home. It's awkward, but we have to reconnect sometime. She'd better not mention Carlito, though.

To keep myself occupied while Mom's inside, I use my phone to search for more about the Popeyes. Everything I find only confirms what I already knew: that they're a nasty bunch playing in a far rougher league than the Annihilators and the Spartans.

"What did Jamie tell you?" Mom asks when she's back and we're walking toward the car. "What's that bruise about?"

I tell her that he isn't giving out details.

"That's all?"

"He's coping," I reply. There's no sense getting her more upset.

"He told me about the lawyer." She reaches out and squeezes my shoulder—her way of thanking me, I guess.

I nod. "Seemed okay that he's getting one but not that excited."

"Did he say anything about getting away from those guys in the club?"

"No."

I know what she wants me to say—that Jamie's vowed to leave the biker life behind—but there's no point telling a big lie and giving her false hope.

She goes quiet but I can guess what she's thinking. Her firstborn child is accused of first-degree murder and there isn't a thing she can do about it. How much lower can we sink?

Chapter
33

For the past few years, football has been my go-to safe place. But gridiron glory isn't on my mind at all right now. As Jamie watches his back in jail and Ripper recovers in the hospital from a gunshot wound, the thought of people in stretchy pants running up and down a field fighting for control of an inflated leather ball just doesn't seem like the biggest thing in the world anymore. In fact, it's hard to think of anything smaller or less important.

I'm also finding it impossible to stop thinking of Brenda. Imagining us together is my new go-to safe place.

"Did you hear about Ripper? I text her. It's Wednesday night and I'm in my bedroom, back at home with Mom, at least for the time being, and I'm going a little stir-crazy.

Part of me is hoping that Brenda knows more about this than I do. I'm sure she's been talking with Carlito, and maybe he has let something slip.

She writes back immediately. She must be restless too. *Yeah WTF? He was shot??*

Gutless drive-by. He's alive. He was hit in the shoulder and side.

Why?

She seems as puzzled about it as me. If Carlito knows anything, I guess he's not sharing it with her.

Imagine he angered the big club. Plus pissed off members of the Annihilators and the Spartans who wanted to join Popeyes.

But who would have done it?

The Popeyes could have directed it, I reply. *That's the obvious answer. Would make it easier to absorb the Annihilators.*

Yeah, but I don't see them screwing it up.

Nobody's perfect.

I meant this as a joke. It's the kind of joke Ripper himself would make. But she does have a point. The Popeyes are good at this sort of thing, and the last few weeks have shown me it doesn't take a genius to end a life.

Ripper's going to be okay? she asks.

Such a hopeful, innocent question.

Looks like it.

Ripper wanted my brother to quit, was pushing Trent to stop cooking. Imagine that—a biker trying to get someone out of the drug business. But Trent kept on doing it, even when the Popeyes shoved their way in. He wanted to buy a house by the lake. Jamie wanted Trent to quit too.

He thought Trent was nuts to be greedy. Wanted him to just leave. Thought that would cool things down.

Hands down, it's the longest text Brenda has ever sent me. I read it twice before replying, to make sure I'm taking it all in. *Leave the club? Leave town?*

Both.

This is news to me. *How do you know that?* I ask.

Trent told me. But I didn't want to move again. I was tired of shuffling around. I'm tired of having to make new friends in school. Now the kids in my grade will be younger than me, which is embarrassing. But I didn't want to hang him out to dry either.

She's in a talkative mood tonight, and obviously feeling a lot of guilt, but her brother was a big boy.

Guess we have to wait for Ripper to explain, she adds, before I have a chance to reply. *If he recovers. And if he talks.*

He'll recover, I text. *But I doubt he'll talk. Too old-school.*

See what you can find out, and maybe call me tomorrow when you get back from the gym?

She knows my gym routine already. Sort of like we are a couple.

Don't think I'll go.

Are you hurt?

No.

I haven't told her about almost being crushed on the bench press the last time I was there. I haven't told anyone.

More important than ever to go to the gym. Should work out harder, not less.

I'm not sure what she's getting at. One day won't make a difference. I can see that she's still typing, so I wait for her to finish.

Don't let people squash your dream. Trent lost his dream of helping our family. Your dream is more solid. Real. It's clean. Don't lose it.

Okay coach. Then: *What's your dream?* It seems like a fair question. The pause that follows feels awkward. Awkward and intimate.

Doesn't matter. Can't turn back the clock.

I don't know how to reply in a way that won't seem like I'm prying. So I just stare out my large attic window at the moon and feel not so alone for a while.

Chapter
34

I'm back at the gym the next morning, Jake at my side. I know Brenda will ask me about it, and I want to be able to tell her that I worked out hard. It's also nice to be hanging out with Jake again.

I've tried not to think about it too much, but it feels like kind of a big deal to be back here. The last time I was here, someone tried to seriously harm me, and that someone is still out there. But the gym is my home-away-from-home, and I'm not about to run away.

"Let's do it," Jake says with no hint of a smile. He's looking around the gym floor like a guard dog. Jake's not used to violence in his life, and there's been enough of it in mine lately to make him feel nervous. My brother is in jail for murder, a biker war is threatening to break out in our quiet little town, and a guy he knows I know is in the hospital, the victim of a drive-by shooting. No wonder he's on edge.

There's no one I'd rather be here with, but it wouldn't kill him to lighten up a little. When Jake's not joking or posing you know there's a problem.

"What's on the program?" he asks.

"No benches or squats. No heavy stuff."

"No spotter stuff?"

"Not today."

With Jake, I don't have to explain. I need to be back in the Zone, where there's no room for panic. I need to feel at home in this place again, but it's going to take some work.

My mind is cycling through these thoughts when I notice Dave Hanson, Jamie's friend from back in the day, on the other side of the room. He's alone and I wonder, just for a second, if he's been sent to meet with me on some kind of undercover mission, thinking I might have information about the violence of the past few days. It wouldn't be the craziest thing to happen this week.

Dave is over at the bench press area when I approach him.

"Want a spot?" I ask.

"Thanks," he says reflexively. Then he sees my face, smiles, and sits up.

"Josh! It's been a while. How's your Mom holding up?"

"Um, as well as can be expected, I guess."

I'm not going to go into details here.

"Say hi to her for me. And to Jamie."

I was just a little kid when he and Jamie hung around together. Sometimes Dave would pick me up and tickle me. Even hold me upside down and make me really squeal. Now I outweigh him by probably fifty pounds.

He does a set of ten reps on the bench press, with me helping on the last three.

"There's something I wanted to ask you about . . . ," I say, once the bar is safely on the rack.

I can see Dave tense up a bit. Whatever friendship he and Jamie had in the past, Dave's a cop now and I'm the brother of an accused killer. This is awkward. If he's working a sting, he's a really good actor.

"It's complicated," I say. "Is there any place . . . ?"

Dave looks around. There are enough people in the weight room that we can't really speak privately here.

"I'll meet you in the sauna in ten minutes," he says.

"Perfect."

It's like a scene from some old gangster movie when I step into the hot room in my towel. An older guy is on his way out as Dave comes in a minute or two after me. It's just us now. I suppose the place could be bugged, but I don't have time to be paranoid. Besides, I have nothing to hide.

"First of all, let's be blunt," I say, trying to sound older and more collected than I am. "I know Jamie didn't do it."

"You're a good brother."

"Seriously, I know."

"With all due respect, you can't know." Dave runs his fingers through his hair and takes a deep breath before speaking again. "I was his friend. He's a great guy. But we both know Jamie has a temper."

I nod. No point arguing the truth.

"It's nice you believe Jamie is innocent but . . ."

"I *know*," I insist. "He wasn't in town. He was in Guelph. He couldn't be in two places at the same time."

"You can prove that?"

"*You* can."

I tell him about the meeting between the Spartans and Annihilators, the top-secret effort to block their clubs from folding into the Popeyes.

"If you know so much, why do you need me?" he asks when I'm done.

"I need to be able to confirm it. I need to know if you guys had one of those Stingrays in operation there."

"Then you don't *really* know," he says, seeing right through the confidence I'd managed to fake up until this point. "You want to believe he was there. I would too, if it were my brother."

He must see the frustration on my face.

"But *you* guys can prove it." I cringe at how shaky my voice sounds, how desperate.

"Us guys?"

"The police . . . with the Stingrays."

"That's not me." He pauses for a moment, then adds: "I have a buddy who deals with that."

He is thinking hard now; he clearly knows more.

"I'm really not supposed to talk about this stuff," he says.

"I just need to know if Stingrays were being used in Guelph that night. I don't need to know exactly what they intercepted. Just if they were operating when Trent was killed in St. Thomas."

Dave takes a deep breath.

"I just need the truth," I say. "Nothing more."

He looks me in the eye, then shifts his gaze up to the ceiling as he lets out a big sigh.

And then he nods his head.

Chapter 35

I call the lawyer the club's recommended, Elaine Lewis, as soon as I get in the car. Within two hours, I'm sitting in her office on Wellington Road in London. It's a little bit of a drive, but that's the last thing on my mind. She's supposed to be good, and I've got to get her going on what I just found out. Her practice is located above the regional headquarters of the Lithuanian-Canadian Association and a cozy restaurant that makes Eastern European comfort food.

Her office is respectable, if less than splashy. There's no fancy art on the walls or supermodel receptionist, like in the movies and TV shows you see about lawyers, but there is a framed photo of Rubin "Hurricane" Carter, a boxer who was wrongly convicted of murder, on the wall. It's signed, "To my good friend, Elaine. Thanks for the good work." There's also a photo of a novice kids' hockey team that includes a smiley girl named Sunny Lewis, presumably Elaine's daughter.

Elaine is a small woman, probably no more than five foot four. She's wearing a blue-and-white striped Oxford-cloth shirt and a blue blazer and her black hair is pulled back tight. There's very little makeup on her face. I don't know why, but the whole sort of severe look is somehow ultra-feminine.

"I'll be upfront with you," Elaine begins, in a matter-of-fact way. I guess she's not so big on small talk, but that's okay with me. "This case will take eighteen months minimum, with pre-trial and trial. That's if we're lucky. The prosecution doesn't like to plea bargain on biker cases these days. Bad optics."

"He's no Popeye," I say, feeling the need to put some distance between my brother and the guys this woman is used to defending.

"Yeah. You know that and I know that but they all look and sound the same to everyone else."

There's something warm about her even though she's using her professional voice.

I tell her about my conversation with Dave in the sauna—leaving out his name—and float out the Stingray idea. "Can we do something with that?" I ask.

"You're the football player, right?"

I'm flattered she knows.

"Yes."

"I believe there's a football play called a Hail Mary."

She's right. A Hail Mary is a long desperation pass—the play the coach pulls out when you have no other options and are trying to win in one big move.

"Yes." I'm not feeling encouraged.

"Those Stingrays? That's Hail Mary stuff. I don't know if it will work, but we can try to subpoena whatever information the police have. Still, we have to be realistic."

She's talking to me like I'm an adult and it's making me queasy.

"I get it that it's an intriguing idea," she continues, and I can hear that warmth creep back into her voice again. "Headlines. Maybe lawsuits. Stirring things up with telecommunications giants who have political connections. Arguments about when the police should be allowed to decrypt private communications. Lawyers love that sort of stuff. But it's far-fetched too. I'm just telling you that it's a long shot. It's a possibility, but I don't want to stake everything on one flashy move. The prosecution wants this to go to trial. They want to look tough on bikers."

She sounds like my coach. He's constantly telling us to do the work. To hope for the best and prepare for the worst. That victory comes from little things. All of that stuff.

Thinking of eighteen months of lawyer fees makes me want to throw up. We can't afford that. Not even close. The pressure is on me to help out with the bill— and I can't do that and play university ball.

I hate Hail Marys. It's what you do when you're losing and are almost out of time.

Chapter
36

The call from Ripper's daughter is unexpected. I answer it in the hallway outside of the lawyer's office, as I'm waiting for the elevator and trying to figure out how to make all of this work.

"He wants to see you," she says. "Can you come by tonight?"

Of course I can. I'll swing by the hospital on the way home.

I meet Frances in a coffee shop in the lobby. We're lucky to find a table among the scores of other hospital visitors. A family on my left is talking about a sick grandfather. On my right, a group is worrying about a boy who's getting his tonsils out. They're all focused on their own problems. I guess the best place to be anonymous is in a crowd.

"He's only supposed to have visits with family," she says. Before I can get upset, she adds, "So come with me. We'll go in together. We're family today, cousin."

She has a great smile, just like her dad. I've always liked Ripper and this feels special, like I'm getting close to something good. I notice a cop's eyes on us as we step onto the elevator.

The first person we see when we get off on Ripper's floor is another cop. She's sitting on a chair outside his room, and I can see the pistol in her holster. I can also see a mic button in her lapel, I guess in case she needs to call for backup.

Frances nods at her and she nods back.

The cop doesn't turn her head when Frances breezes by with me, although her eyes do follow me. I don't think we fooled her.

Ripper appears to be in a state of semi-sleep when we enter the room. There's a tube coming out of his arm and another particularly nasty-looking one in his nose. His room has an antiseptic smell. It feels so strange to see Ripper in this environment, where he's not in control. Somehow it's even more disconcerting to see all of the flowers at his bedside. I've never associated Ripper with floral arrangements. There's also a balloon bouquet and a few get-well cards, ranging from a sentimental one with a sunset on the front to a goofy one of a dog riding a motorcycle that says, "Only a biker knows why a dog sticks his head out of the window."

I don't notice anything from the club.

Frances gently taps her father's arm, then kisses his cheek.

"Hi, Dad," she says.

He smiles gently and his eyes tear up a little. Maybe he was having a bad dream. This isn't the Ripper I'm used to.

"I brought Josh," she says.

"Do you have a minute to talk?" I say.

"That depends," he replies. "Have you been talking to my doctor? She's the expert on how much time I have."

Frances rolls her eyes. Same old Ripper.

Ripper turns onto his side to face me and his eyes open wider.

"Glad you could come," he says, his voice a raspy whisper. "You bring me that coffee, finally?" He cracks a little grin. "It must be cold by now."

I don't know how to answer this, and it doesn't matter.

Ripper lowers his voice, my signal to lean in a little closer.

"Sorry again about your brother. He's a solid guy."

I just nod. Ripper's a class act. Here he is, full of tubes and sporting a bullet hole or two and he's passing on his sympathies about my situation and trying to make me proud of my delinquent brother. No wonder Jamie likes him so much.

"So you're trying to help him?" Ripper says. "You're a good brother. I had hoped it wouldn't come to this but obviously things have gotten pretty serious."

I'm not sure if he's talking about his situation or

Jamie's. Maybe he means that they're connected. But if so, how?

"You remember that guy Jamie was hanging around with at Trollop's party? The Anglo guy from Quebec?"

I recall Jamie introducing me to a husky guy who seemed to be keeping his distance from the other Quebec bikers, yes. He struck me as a bit of a throw-back. Lots of tattoos on his arms and wild, long hair. He looked more like a partier than a master criminal.

"Yeah. I didn't really talk to the guy but I remember him."

"That's Tom McCrae from the South Shore Popeyes in Montreal. You need to find him."

"Why?"

"He's Jamie's alibi. He and Jamie were hanging out together in Guelph the night Trent was shot. There's no way he could have done it."

"How do you know?"

"Because I kidded him about it. They had a bet. Your brother lost fifty bucks on that game. It was on TV in the sports bar where they were hanging. He picked the Argonauts to win, and Montreal took it. Last-minute interception."

Ripper smiles at the memory.

"That's great!" This seems too good to be true. "But how can we prove it?"

"Tom took a selfie with Jamie after the game with the TV and the scoreboard in the background. He told me about it the next day on the phone. He was laughing. Jamie was teasing him and then the Argos blew it with a minute left. The Alouettes won it with a Hail Mary."

I like football as much as anyone, but I don't particularly care about how the game was won right now, just that Jamie and McCrae went to it. If I can prove it, Brenda will know that it's not just a theory that Jamie didn't kill Trent. It's the truth.

"Get that photo and Jamie goes free," Ripper tells me. "He couldn't be in two places at once. You'll need to ask McCrae in person, though. I don't think he'll trust you over the phone."

"Any idea how I'd find him?"

"This is embarrassing. I've lost track of time. What day is it?"

I update him.

"There's a party in Toronto tomorrow night," Ripper says. "Friday. In Riverdale. You know the Spartans' clubhouse there?"

I know of the place, but I've never been inside. "I can find it," I assure him quickly. I have other questions to ask. "Why wouldn't Jamie have told the police where he was?"

Ripper shoots me a look like I should know better.

"He's no rat. He's not about to tell club business to the cops."

"But it's a murder charge!" I exclaim.

Ripper ignores me. "There's a good chance McCrae'll

be at the party. He's not the type of guy to turn down an invitation."

"I'll go."

"Be careful," he warns me.

"I'll just say I'm Jamie's brother."

"Seriously. Be very careful. Someone obviously has it in for your brother. You don't know who's who in the zoo. No one does anymore. I sure don't. Tom is a good enough guy but he's pissed off some serious people."

"Who's angry at him?"

"Who isn't? Some Spartans. Some Popeyes."

"Why?"

I can't believe I'm asking—outsiders aren't entitled to inquire about club business—so I'm even more surprised when Ripper answers.

"Tom's going around trying to talk people on all sides out of the merger. He doesn't think the Popeyes should join with either the Spartans or the Annihilators."

"Why does he care?"

"He's old-school. He's not so big on the business. He doesn't like how corporate the Popeyes are becoming. He wants fun. He wants it to be 1967 forever. He likes the idea of small clubs and big parties."

"So shouldn't he be keeping a low profile? That guy from the Nomads keeps sniffing around—Baker the Undertaker."

Ripper raises an eyebrow at that. I can tell he's surprised that I even know the guy's name, but I'm past caring. And I guess he is too, because he keeps going.

"You'd think. But no. McCrae's the type of guy to run at a problem, not away from it."

There's a long pause as Ripper sips some water from a straw. "He didn't ride his bike down here, though. He's driving a white F-150 with a rabbit's foot hanging from the mirror. With Quebec plates, obviously."

All at once, Ripper sounds tired. Frances gives me a look that say it's time to go.

I thank Ripper for the lead, feeling a bit light-headed as I stand to leave. It's been a busy day—cops and lawyers and now Ripper. So much has happened, and although I don't want to get my hopes up, I feel closer to freeing Jamie right now than I have since this whole mess started. I just have to find Tom and see if he's willing to admit being with my brother the night that Trent was killed. One more day and the drama could be over.

I say my good-byes and head for the elevator. On the ride down to the main floor, I think of calling Jamie's lawyer and filling her in, but decide to hold off. Nothing's definite yet, and I hear lawyers bill you in fifteen-minute blocks, every time you call. Besides, I get the feeling she already thinks I'm a little naive and I don't want to reinforce that.

I text Brenda when I get to the car. *Heading out of town for a little while.*

This time, she replies instantly.

Where? Why?

Toronto. Hoping for new info.

Seriously? You have to go?

Yup.

Be careful. Promise.

It's not the first time she's sounded nervous about something I'm doing, or worried about me. I could get used to this.

For sure.

Going to be quiet around here. Carlito just headed out of town too.

Great. I wonder where's he going, and what for? Just one more thing to worry about.

Chapter
37

The Spartans' clubhouse in Toronto is a grubby local landmark of sorts. I've never actually been inside but I've seen it on the news. Every Christmas they stick a big sign on their roof with Santa on a Harley hauling his sled.

The two-story brick house is in an area that used to be pretty tough, I've been told, but it looks like the neighborhood has gotten trendy. There are Audis and Volvos in the driveways of newly renovated homes, and $2,000 bicycles locked up outside restaurants and storefronts on the main streets.

Sometimes guys from this club ride down to Annihilator parties in St. Thomas, so I know a few of them a little bit. Luckily, one of them is on the street dismounting from his motorcycle as I pull up outside.

"Hey bro, sorry about your brother," he says when he spots me.

"Thanks, appreciate it."

"You're welcome to party with us tonight."

And with that, I'm allowed inside. There are black leather couches and a huge TV in the living room. On the walls are framed club photos. There's also a cuckoo clock that an engraved sign tells me is a gift from some club in Germany.

To the rear of the house is a bar that leads out to the fenced backyard, and that's where most of the party seems to be going on. I also see a door to what must be a VIP room, shielded by a black curtain and marked "Members only."

The bar is long and made of hardwood and has the club crest carved right into it. The Rolling Stones' "Miss You" is playing at top volume. It's a little sad and a little sexy and seems to fit the mood. There's a stripper pole near the bar and a woman is spinning around it, doing her best to interpret the song. She's wearing black workout gear, though I'm not sure how long that will last.

I buy a beer and head out to the backyard. Jamie's supposed alibi, the Popeye named Tom, is nowhere to be seen, and I didn't see a white Ford truck on the street. I don't know what to do other than wait for him to show up.

The music's pretty loud in the backyard too, but I imagine the neighbors know better than to complain too much. The bikers were here before the yuppies moved in.

I recognize two more guys in the backyard and nod in their direction.

"Sorry about your brother," one of them says.

My brother's bad fortune seems to have given me a certain status.

I sip my beer and try to relax. The guys here seem pretty loose tonight. There's a lot of laughter ringing out, and some good-natured kidding going on. I wonder why Tom hasn't shown up yet. Could he have feared some sort of ambush at the party or was he just not interested? Maybe he's at home in Montreal and I'm wasting my time. But it's not even midnight yet, so there's a chance he'll still come.

I can see inside the clubhouse from here and notice that the woman on the pole is considerably less dressed than she was when I passed through. There are a half dozen other women mingling in the crowd who look like they might also have polished a pole in the not-so-distant past. Some guys on a couch are snorting something and giggling crazily.

I turn around and drift farther into the backyard. I'm doing my best to fit into the party vibe but I don't want another beer. The last thing I need is to be drunk if Jamie's friend shows up, and anyway, I'm an athlete, not a biker.

Besides the Spartans that I've spoken to already, there are a dozen or so guys from other clubs that I recognize. There's also a dorky-looking guy wearing a brand-new vest that announces him as a member of the Roadrunners, a club from Barrie, a small city north of Toronto. He's strutting around with his chest puffed out like a bantam rooster.

"Hey bro, can you get me a beer?" one of the Spartans I spoke to asks him.

"Do I look like your waiter?"

The Roadrunner's words hang in the air, clear and crisp and defiant and begging for a reaction.

"Excuse me?" answers the Spartan.

Whenever a biker gets ultra-polite, there's a very good chance things are going to get dangerous.

"I said, 'Do I look like your waiter?'"

With that, the dorky biker smiles at two women standing nearby. One of them smiles back. The smarter one looks down and away.

Everyone seems to be listening now. There are a couple of nervous giggles and plenty of people trying not to stare.

The Spartan and the buddy he's standing with are enjoying the audience. They whisper back and forth and then one of them leaves the backyard in a rush. His friend smiles to himself for a moment and whistles into his empty beer can, still standing un-comfortably close to the back-talking Roadrunner. Then his friend returns with a length of blue nylon rope in his hands. That can't be good.

"Come over here."

It's the Spartan who asked for the beer, addressing the rooster.

It's not a request, but it's ignored nonetheless.

"I said, 'Come over here,'" he repeats.

Still the smaller man ignores him, so the Spartan gets right in his face, smiling in a crazy narrow grimace. He grabs the uppity Roadrunner around the waist, cool and confident, as if this is the most natural thing in the world, then pins the man's arms to his side.

That's when the second Spartan forces the rope around his neck from behind.

Neither Spartan is smiling now, and the Roadrunner looks terrified.

I'm terrified too, and I'm just watching.

Next, the rope is thrown over a low-hanging tree branch and yanked tight.

The gasp from the Roadrunner is the most sickening thing I have ever heard.

Now the two friends are hauling on the rope, hoisting the smaller man into the air. It's like they're doing a farmyard chore. The Roadrunner tries to free himself, but the rope is cutting tightly into his neck. He's flapping his arms like a real rooster and his face is a sickening shade of purple.

It seems like someone should call 911, but I'm too shocked to move. Instead, I just stare. It's the first lynching I've ever seen—or even heard of—in the biker world, and it's enough to cause the Roadrunner to wet his pants.

After what seems like an eternity, the two Spartans

let go of the rope and the Roadrunner collapses to the ground. No one rushes up to see if he's okay.

A few seconds later, he starts to gasp and sputter, and I feel an enormous sense of relief. It's a miracle that his neck isn't broken.

The two Spartans look in his direction and smile. Then they look at me.

I decide it's time to go. It's late and it's pretty clear Jamie's friend isn't coming.

He must have gone back to Montreal. If I want his help I'll have to follow him there.

Chapter
38

In biker circles, Quebec is known as the "Red Zone." Red's the color of heat and the color of blood and it seems fitting that the Red Zone is the home base of the Popeyes, whose members love red vests.

They don't play around in Quebec. Bill says that the sky's the limit here for anyone smart enough or tough enough to take advantage of the smuggling potential that the city's ocean access and proximity to the massive New York market afford.

I drive overnight to Montreal in search of the white Ford F-150 and Tom McCrae, and get to the clubhouse, in the city's suburban South Shore neighborhood, around seven in the morning. It's pretty hard to miss since it has a Popeyes flag flying from the front gate.

I don't really have a plan for finding Tom but the clubhouse seems like the place to start. It's surrounded by a wrought-iron fence topped with razor wire and is set back from the street on a little hill. Anyone without a battering ram will need to be buzzed inside.

I'm too dozy and tired to make any decisions, so I pull into the parking lot of a nearby chicken restaurant and spend the next four hours sleeping in the car. When I wake up I'm a little more alert, so I take another pass of the clubhouse. Still nothing promising. I think about waiting for a bit and then driving by one more time, then decide against it. There are security cameras covering the area and I don't need to arouse suspicion.

But I didn't drive all the way here to sit around and wait. I tell the butterflies in my stomach to settle down as I slowly ease my car up to the intercom by the gate. I roll down the window and press the button.

"Oui?"

"Bonjour," I reply. With that, I've pretty well exhausted my French vocabulary, unless I can work "deluxe" or "bon" into the conversation.

"Hello," the voice tries again. He's heard me say one word and can already tell I don't speak the language.

"Hello. My brother is Jamie from the Annihilators in Ontario. I need to find a friend of his, Tom McCrae."

"Wait there," an abrupt voice orders.

Five minutes later, a Cadillac coupe comes down the hill from the clubhouse. It's a fine car, a two-door sporty CTS model, but I reckon there's still room in

the trunk for a body or two. The man getting out of
the driver's side can't be more than thirty. He looks
plenty tough but he's not wearing club colors, so
maybe he's just a prospect. They get most of the menial
grunt jobs, but they're also often the most violent and
unpredictable, since they're constantly trying to prove
themselves. He's clearly wary of me.

"Your brother's name?"

"Jamie Williams. St. Thomas Annihilators."

"I don't mean to be rude, but do you have some
identification? Something to prove you are who you
say you are?"

I pull out my wallet, which I open to show my
driver's license. My hand is a little shaky when I pass
it to him.

He nods.

"Take off your jacket and hand it to me."

I oblige. I wonder what he'd do if I said no.

Part of me—a big part—just wants to run.

"Turn around."

I know that bikers sometimes keep their handguns
in the small of their back, tucked into their jeans. He's
checking for that.

"All the way around."

I obey and he seems more relaxed.

"Hop in."

I climb into the passenger side of the Caddy, and
in a minute we're at the clubhouse. He buzzes at the

door. It's metal, painted red, with a couple of cameras over it and a little peephole drilled in at eye level. An aggressive buzz answers his and he opens the door. It makes a heavy thud when it closes behind us. I won't be getting out until somebody decides I should be getting out. Hopefully, I'm still in one happy piece when that happens.

This clubhouse is incredibly clean. There's a pool table on the main floor, impressively painted in the club's black and gold, and a half dozen arcade games against one wall. There's also a massive stainless-steel fridge, and lots of framed photos of bikers on the walls. It doesn't have the frat-house feel of the Spartans' clubhouse, and it's miles ahead of Trollop's barn and the Annihilators' dump in downtown St. Thomas. The prospect steps back as someone else takes charge of things.

"So you want to see Tom?"

The person speaking is about forty-five and has clearly spent time in a weight room. He has a shaved head and a goatee and looks like the kind of guy who says things like, "Are you gonna biker up or lie there and bleed?"

"Yes. It's about my brother."

He doesn't seem to want to hear any details, just hands me a piece of cardboard torn from a cigarette box. On it is a phone number.

"Call this," he says.

I get out my phone and do as he says.

To my surprise, Tom picks up at the other end. I recognize his voice from our introduction at Trollop's.

He doesn't ask how I got the number. Clearly, someone he trusts trusts me.

"Have you eaten yet?" Tom asks.

I tell him I could use another meal.

"Meet me at Jordan's Diner, down McDougall Street from the clubhouse. I'll be there in thirty minutes."

And then he hangs up.

I'm driven back down the hill, and as I'm getting into the Cruze, I see Baker the Undertaker pulling up in a Hummer. He sees me but doesn't stop to talk. That's fine with me. The less I have to do with him the better.

Chapter
39

The diner Tom's directed me to is kind of folksy and charming, specializing in coffee and comfort food, but there's definitely an edge to it. Near the front door is a bulletin board bearing pictures of trucks and motorcycles for sale, and there's a nice selection of Western belt buckles by the cash register. It's the sort of establishment where the serving staff don't suffer from a lack of confidence, and I'm guessing no one would be surprised to hear that the cooks learned their trade in a prison somewhere.

I pick a booth by the window so I can see the parking lot. In a few minutes, a white Ford truck pulls up. As it gets closer, I can see a rabbit's foot hanging from the rearview mirror.

I immediately recognize the driver. When I saw Tom McCrae at the party, I thought he looked like he could be a good fullback, if he ever got in shape.

His shoulders are massive but he also has a sizable paunch.

Once he gets to my table, he reaches out to shake my hand biker-style, our two thumbs interlocked, just like the first time we met, and gives me a friendly pat on the shoulder with his other hand.

"I'm a popular guy these days," he says.

"How do you mean?"

"Heard another guy from Ontario is in town asking about me. Guy with the fancy cowboy boots."

"Carlito?"

"That's him. I don't answer a lot of the calls I get but you're Jamie's brother and that's good enough for me."

I don't push him. I just want the photo of Jamie. He can sort out the rest of the drama himself.

"You came all this way to see me?" As he speaks, he nods in the direction of a nearby waiter, signaling that we'd like to order. My stomach growls. Butterflies or not, I guess I'm hungry.

"I need to help my brother. I'm sure you've heard what's going on."

He nods, and the expression on his face suggests genuine concern. But then again, I'm tired and maybe he's just a good actor. To be honest, I'm having trouble trusting anyone these days.

"He's super-proud of you. Says you work out a lot. Hard."

"As much as I can."

"I like the gym too."

On one of his pumped-up arms is an expensive-looking gold watch engraved with the Popeyes crest.

"Not enough to just work out," Tom adds. "Have to work out smart."

"I do," I say.

"If you ever want a little something, I can get it to you," Tom says.

I'm guessing he's talking about steroids, or maybe human growth hormones. I've stayed away from that stuff so far, and plan on keeping it that way.

"Thanks, but I'm okay."

The waitress comes by and pours us both a coffee. As we order our omelets, I'm aware that McCrae's eyes are following everyone coming into and leaving the place.

"Did the cops question you?" Tom asks me.

"Yeah. I was in the station for a bit. They asked where I was that night. How I knew Trent."

"And?"

"I told the truth but I didn't say much. I wasn't with Jamie around the time it happened. I didn't know Trent except to say 'hi.'"

"They didn't go hard on you?"

"No. One of the cops was the father of a kid I play football with. He must know I'm not in the club. I go to the occasional party but that's it."

"Have the cops said anything else about Jamie's charges? Released any details about what they suspect?"

"They said Trent was killed on the night you were hanging out with Jamie."

"How did you know about that?" he snaps.

For the first time since we've sat down, Tom seems less than friendly, angry even. I don't know what to make of his tone, and I'm too tired to give it much more thought. If I want his help, I have to be honest with him.

"Ripper."

Now he smiles. "How's Ripper doing? Getting better?"

So he knows about the attack.

"Getting better. Not quickly, but getting better."

Tom drinks his coffee in silence. If he has a theory about why Ripper was targeted, he's not volunteering to share it with me.

Time to get to my point. "Ripper told me you and Jamie were together that night," I begin, wondering how to say what I need to say next. I don't even know what I'm asking for, just that Tom's my only hope. "I know you can't say too much about what you were doing, and I don't want to get you in trouble with any-one . . ." I take a deep breath, trying to calm myself down. Did I actually just say "get you in trouble"? This isn't some schoolyard fight, and we're not six-year-olds. I give my head a small shake, trying to dislodge the cobwebs so I can focus. "I guess I'm just wonder-ing if you know anything that might help. Or if you'd be willing to tell the cops that you were with him, and that he couldn't have done what they think he did to Trent." A deep breath, and then I add: "Ripper told me that you and Jamie took a photo, with the big-screen TV and the Argos game in the background. That the picture showed the score right after the game."

"I wanted to be able to tease Jamie about it," he says, warming to the memory. "Easiest fifty bucks I ever made."

"Can I see it? It could be all it takes to get Jamie freed. Could you . . . ?"

"Happy to help for Jamie. My phone's in my truck. I'll be back in a second."

"Want me to go out with you?"

"Finish your coffee. Don't want them clearing out our food. I hate it when they take away the plate before I'm finished."

"I'll guard it with my life."

He jumps to his feet, showing off that he's a man of action, I guess. As Tom heads for the door, I look around for cops. We aren't doing anything illegal, but somehow I'm nervous anyway.

This has been so easy. I've been dealing with drama for so long now that I'm not sure how to take the fact that it's almost over. In a minute, Tom's going to walk through that door and serve up the evidence that can clear my brother's name, all as I'm sitting here eating comfort food.

BOOM!

The noise—a massive, solid wall of sound—comes from out in the parking lot.

The waitress lets out a scream.

Outside, a woman is shrieking hysterically.

There's a cloud of smoke coming from the area where McCrae's truck is parked. I dart out the door and am running toward his vehicle when I see something lying on the pavement near the mangled front end of the truck. It's a cell phone, crushed and burned almost beyond recognition. And there's something else a few feet away. It's a flashy gold watch . . . attached to a human hand.

Chapter
40

That bloody hand . . . that watch. The sound of the explosion. I can't get any of it out of my head during the long drive home. We had just been talking . . . Now Tom's dead and Jamie . . . Jamie may be heading off to prison for a long, long time.

Is this my fault?

Did the Popeyes use me to set up Tom? They gave me his number. He mentioned not trusting phone calls. He was an obstacle to the Popeyes' plans to expand into St. Thomas, and maybe someone made this clear to the club's higher-ups. Carlito? Some brotherhood.

If I'd gone out to the truck with him, I'd probably be dead too.

I check my messages at a rest stop an hour or so down the highway and see a text from Brenda and another from Jake.

Things good? Brenda has asked.

Hearing from her is great—especially now—but it's unsettling too, given what's happened, and what's still happening. How am I supposed to answer? I wonder if she sends Carlito messages asking after his well-being. I know that she doesn't owe me anything, and we haven't made each other any promises. Hell, we've barely spent any time together. But still . . .

On my way home, I reply. Then I add a happy face.

For the first time since the night of Jamie's arrest, I'm really scared. An hour or so ago I thought I was in control—that I was winning. Now Tom McCrae is dead and it was me who drew him out into a public place where he'd be vulnerable. And so far, all the violence—Trent, Ripper, the weird incident at the gym—has gone unpunished. This stuff is for real.

And I don't even have the photo. This trip has been a massive failure.

Glad you're safe, Brenda replies.

I almost laugh out loud. Her concern is nice, but safe feels like the farthest thing from what I am. I consider asking her about Carlito, but I don't want to blow the mood—or give anything away—by bringing up his name.

Thanks. See you soon.

I don't know much about women, but Jamie has told me more than once that sometimes shutting up is the best way to go. I add another happy face before sending the message, then look at Jake's text.

How have you been? he asked.

Complicated. Been out of town, I text back.

Missed you at the gym, he replies immediately.

An image of being at the gym—of working out with nothing but football on my mind—rushes into my head. For a moment, it's all I can think about. I want to be there so badly that I can feel the ache in my gut. I want to go back to a time when the biggest worry I had was whether or not I was going to get a scholarship so I could run around on a football field. To a time when Jake and I were in grade nine, watching *Ghostbusters* at his place and munching on popcorn. To a time before Trent was killed and Jamie was arrested and I was hanging out with guys who get blown up. I want to go back to the barbecue and dance with Brenda, and forget about everything that's happened since. Besides, it's sad to think of Jake at the gym alone. Who would listen to his jokes?

Let me know if I can help, he writes next.

I know he means it.

When I get back to town, I'll tell him face to face about Tom and the bomb and the hand and the watch, though I might stop short of admitting that I'm worried Tom's murder was partly my fault. And I probably won't tell him how much he means to me, but I hope he senses that.

I'm about to get back on the road when a text arrives from Elaine, Jamie's lawyer. She tells me to be in court first thing Monday morning, and that my mother needs to be there too. Just as well I never told her about my road trip, and it's lucky I'll be back in St. Thomas in time.

Be there, she has written. *Seriously.*

Chapter
41

I can't remember the last time I saw Jamie so nervous. He's actually sweating as he talks with Elaine at their table near the front of the courtroom. When the bailiff instructs everyone to rise, they both stand up. Jamie rocks from side to side for a few moments, then takes a deep breath and stands perfectly still.

It's a small courtroom and the only journalist there is Julie, a reporter from the *Sun-Sentinel* who I barely know. She gives me a little nod, as if she knows something big is about to happen.

"Bill said I should be here," she says, "but I don't know what to expect."

Bill does have his sources.

Mom picks up on the tension. She's sitting beside me in the front row of the gallery, dressed very properly in a skirt and a jacket I've only seen her wear at funerals. She's trying hard, which counts for something, I guess. She's digging her fingernails into my forearm, which actually hurts a bit, but I don't have the heart to tell her to stop. Even though I've been back at home, we haven't cleared the air about Carlito. It will have to wait. I'm not about to abandon her now.

Elaine walks over to the prosecutor and they lean toward each other, talking quietly so no one else can hear. Then she nods her head, smiles, and steps back to the defendant's table and Jamie.

The prosecutor clears his throat and addresses the judge directly.

"Your Honor, the prosecution wishes to drop the charges against the defendant, Jamie Williams."

Mom gasps then starts to shake. Her fingernails are threatening to break my skin now, but I don't care.

"On what grounds?"

"New evidence, Your Honor."

It's such a short, sweet statement.

I feel like I could fall off my seat.

Mom's crying huge gasping sobs of relief. Jamie is blinking a little, but he's trying to look cool. He turns and smiles at me, holding my gaze for a few long moments. There are tears in his eyes and I can see that he's trembling.

Elaine shakes his hand and gives him a pat on the shoulder.

It's like I'm dreaming.

"Mr. Williams, you are free to go," the judge says.

The whole scene has taken less than ten minutes.

"You couldn't have told us in advance?" I say to Elaine.

I'm joking, but not really.

"You never know until it actually happens," she replies. She looks a bit overwhelmed herself. Then she gives me a hug, which catches me off guard.

"Congratulations!" she says. "You did it!"

"Did what?"

I'm not being sarcastic.

I didn't get anything from Tom that could clear Jamie's name, and I might actually have gotten him killed. What exactly did I do right?

"None of this would have happened without you," Elaine insists.

Mom looks proud and hugs me too. Maybe she thinks I'm being modest. Stunned is more like it.

"The Stingray idea," Elaine says when she realizes I'm not playing dumb, and that I really don't have a clue what she means. "I talked about it with the prosecutor. He's not a bad guy. We've done cases together before. He got the police to check into it. Jamie's phone was picked up in Guelph by the Stingrays at the time of Trent's death. Some of his conversations had even been transcribed. There's some talk about him and a friend watching the football game on TV in Guelph the night of the murder."

"The prosecution caved that quickly?"

"They appreciated the heads-up. It would have been embarrassing for them if this had gone to court. Jamie was nowhere near St. Thomas at the time of the murder and the Stingray records prove it. Citizens' rights groups and the news media would have eaten them alive and there could even have been a lawsuit. This way it goes away quietly until they get the right guy."

The prosecutor reaches out to shake Jamie's hand as we're talking. To my relief, Jamie returns the gesture. He still has the black eye and could easily put one on the prosecutor, if he wanted. Maybe he has grown up a little in jail.

"Smart brother you have there," the prosecutor says to Jamie. "He'll do something after football."

"Don't puff up his head," Jamie says with just a hint of a stutter. "His helmet is tight enough already."

Everyone's smiling, except for Baker the Undertaker, who I've noticed is lurking in the back of the courtroom. I'm not sure when he arrived and wonder how he even heard about the hearing. He leaves without talking to us.

We're walking out to the Cruze when my phone rings. It's the city editor at the *Sun-Sentinel*.

"I was just talking with Julie," he says. "She filled me in. Congratulations."

I'm still in a happy fog.

"Your job's ready when you are," he continues.

"Can I get back to you in a couple of days?" I feel like I need time to absorb everything that's happened.

He sounds a little surprised, but says it's fine.

And that's that. Jamie's a free man and I'm officially un-fired.

Chapter
42

The diner by the tattoo shop is where Jamie and I have our brothers-only celebration the next morning. Pancakes and sausages and plenty of syrup for Jamie and a Western omelet for me.

I don't tell Jamie about seeing Carlito at our house. Why ruin a great day? I also don't want Jamie charged with another murder, one he'd clearly be guilty of. Just joking, sort of.

Jamie treats me to breakfast. He owes me and we both know it.

"Why were you arguing with Trent that night? I know you wanted him to quit cooking, but why did things get so hot?" I've earned the right to know.

Jamie must think so too, because he answers me right away. "He was greedy. Things might have cooled off all around if he just got out of town fast. We offered him some money, some get-lost money. He took it too.

Then he started playing footsie with the Popeyes. He just wouldn't go away and he wouldn't give back the money."

This is club business and confidential: I'm happy that he's treating me like a man, not like a little brother. The club and its rules aren't looking so great at the moment anyway.

"He had made enough," Jamie says. "Having him around was making things dangerous for himself and for the club. Attracting heat from the cops and the Popeyes and even the Spartans. I think you know there are two sides to the club: the Ripper side and the Trollop side, the normal side and the nutbar side. He was helping the nutbar side, the guys who want to join up with the Popeyes."

Then Jamie's voice drops so I can barely hear it and he leans forward.

"I was trying to help him, even though he wasn't being straight with us. Warn him. He was becoming a target. A few of the Spartans thought if they took him out it would make the Annihilators less attractive to the Popeyes. And I heard some of the Popeyes wanted to take him out, too. Just to show they should be taken seriously and not strung along. And some of the Annihilators wanted him out because they wanted everyone to know it's not cool to change sides and play games. It seemed like it was going to be a race to see who could rub him out first." Jamie pauses for a minute and pushes his pancakes around on the plate with his fork. When he speaks again, his voice is tired and sad. "He thought I was being nasty when I told him to get lost. I was the only friend he had but I couldn't convince him of that."

"What did the Popeyes think he had done wrong?"

"He was trying to negotiate. Threatening to go away and not cook for them if they wouldn't pay him enough. There was even a rumor he was selling his recipe to guys connected to other clubs."

"But aren't there plenty of cooks?"

"He was a really good one. And they were probably losing him anyway, so why not make an example out of him for being too greedy? That way, others fall into line."

Jamie leans back in his chair and shakes his head. He may be regretting that he's told me so much, and I'm guessing my window for asking questions is about to close. I decide to get one more in.

"Why couldn't you just have told the police you had an alibi?"

He owes me an answer here too.

He sighs, looks at me, and takes a deep breath.

"The Popeyes have friends everywhere. You'd be surprised. I bet they even have allies in the prosecutor's office and in our own police force. Seriously. They're bigger than they look. I needed it to be known that I'm solid. Otherwise, I'd have been dead in jail. Everyone knew there was at least one rat somewhere in the club. I didn't need people thinking it was me. It's not. And I wasn't going to rat out anybody who was at the Guelph meeting, either, including Tom McCrae."

Jamie's eyes get watery. I'd visited him as soon as I got back from Montreal to tell him about Tom. It was a hard conversation to have, and it's still hard to see my brother upset.

"He's a—he was a brave man." He's fighting his stutter now. "He was taking a risk for me. He was solid."

That's as much as I'll get from him. I get it, I think.

"I know I haven't been the best big brother recently," Jamie says.

It's a pretty huge understatement but I let it go. I know it isn't easy for him to admit this at all.

"I've got some decisions to make," he continues.

Hopefully, this means he'll be more of a drywaller and less of a biker in the future. He might not be on anyone's hit list at the moment, but that could change quickly. Now would be a good time to bail on the biker life, if you ask me.

I glance down at my phone.

Brenda's name is on my call display, along with her photo.

Jamie's smiling at me when I look up again, like a proud big brother.

"You should call her," he says. "She's a keeper."

Chapter
43

Brenda doesn't pick up when I call back. That's okay; there's something I want to do before I see her anyway.

I meet Jake that afternoon with plans to spill some serious sweat in the gym. It'll be the first time I've lifted with a spotter since the day of the incident on the bench press.

As we begin, Jake hikes his shorts up ridiculously high.

"You know how you know I'm going to do some good work today?" he asks, speaking in a deep, affected voice.

He's trying to do some accent, but I have no clue which one. He's totally pleased with it, however.

"I've got on my short shorts. That's how you know."

Jake also has a little ghetto blaster with him. He cranks up "King Kunta" and we get down to it.

What follows is ninety minutes of jock talk and hard work and dumb jokes and all of it feels totally necessary. It's focused exercise punctuated by Jake striking bodybuilder poses, doing his gorilla walk, and reviving the rest of his greatest hits. At one point, he hikes up his shirt, flexes his chest, and says, "Welcome to Twin Peaks." Then he nods at his arms and announces, "Sun's out, guns out." While we're working our legs, he points to his quadriceps and says, "Please stand back—way back—and let Quad-zilla through."

At one particularly tough point in our routine, Jake gives me an earnest look and says, "The secret is to keep breathing."

I can't tell if he's joking.

He pauses a moment, then adds: "We will make it through this if we breathe."

I can't argue with that.

Chapter 44

That evening, I head back to the newsroom. I'd told the city editor I wanted a day or two, but sometime during my workout, I realized that I wanted to go back in, to do normal things.

I'm surprised by how good it feels to be on the job again.

It's particularly nice to see Bill Taylor and his *Illegitimi non carborundum* sign.

"Welcome back!" he says, standing up to give me a quick embrace. He's genuinely happy. Then he adds: "Rather have you as a colleague than a source. You're kind of both now."

"Yup," is the best I can muster. "What are you working on?"

Neither of us wants to waste much time with small talk.

"Was going to ask what you think. A body was

found in a vehicle by a field, about twenty minutes down the road from Trollop's farm."

"When?"

"Early this morning. Victim's white, in his thirties, and heavily tattooed. He was shot in the head. Name's Wally Parkinson."

He can see me shudder.

"I know him."

For the next few minutes, I tell Bill what I know about Wally and explain how he was hanging tight with Trollop at the party where I reconnected with Brenda. He and Jamie definitely weren't close, although they would have called each other "brother."

"He was the prime suspect in Ripper's shooting," Bill tells me.

I'm not shocked to hear this. Prospects like Wally are often willing to do crazy things to earn brownie points with the club. Wally was also an enthusiastic meth user. Big surprise that he screwed up the hit.

"Anything else?"

"His body was found in a stolen Ford truck."

"Green?"

Bill nods.

"Do they think Wally killed Trent?" I ask. I assume the murders must be connected. How can they not be?

"Nope. He was picked up for drunk driving that night. He had a perfect alibi. Idiot luck."

"He's no thinker."

"Exactly. He's Trollop's guy. Ripper was in the way of the club getting closer to the Popeyes, so there's your motive."

"So who killed Wally?"

"Working theory is that Trollop ordered Wally to do the hit on Ripper. Then Trollop turned on him and killed him when it didn't work out."

"Then who killed Trent?" After all that's happened, it still doesn't seem like I'm any closer to knowing.

"It'll be hard to prove unless someone rolls. Don't have a solid identification but the talk is that the guy who took out Trent is someone local."

"Not Baker the Undertaker?"

"Nope. I've learned a few things from some cell phone chatter that's been picked up here and there." He doesn't go into details about his sources, and I don't ask. "Apparently, it was supposed to be a double hit. The secondary target wasn't there when he killed the cook."

"Secondary target?" I can feel a nervous tingle creeping up my spine.

"They keep saying 'she' on their intercepts. Or 'the girl.' Or 'sister.' The cops know who she is but they're having a problem locating her."

The nervous tingle turns to full-blown panic in a nanosecond. He doesn't have to say Brenda's name.

"Why kill her?" I'm sure my voice sounds like a plea.

I text Brenda furiously as we're talking.

"She might have heard things from her brother.

They know she was brought in for questioning and that she was in the police station for quite a while."

No reply from Brenda.

I call her.

Just voicemail.

Brenda has trouble keeping her phone charged, I tell myself. But what Bill says next causes my entire body to tighten.

"Do you know the name Carlito? I'd never heard of him until today. It's an alias or something?"

"What? Where does he fit in?" I ask when I can speak again. I'm sure my voice is cracking.

"The name's come up a few times. Some young guy? He apparently did a ton of time in juvie for some very serious stuff that not many people know about because he was underage and the records were sealed." Bill's shuffling through some papers now.

Carlito, violent? He's always struck me as harmless, a poser who's about talk and image—those stupid boots—not action.

"Oh, here," he says, reading from a typewritten page. "The cops have him as a possible suspect for the cook. Tough, ambitious, and with a very violent past. The cook trusted him, apparently, so he would have been able to get close. The word is that the big club wants him to do another dirty job and then he'll be a full patch Popeye."

I'm shaking now. Have I been completely wrong about this guy?

"The latest is that he went to Quebec a couple of days ago for a face-to-face meeting with the Popeyes' leadership," Bill says. "Probably told to finish the job he started, to take out the secondary target."

Secondary target? Can a life really be reduced to such a bland term? I bet he also reported on Tom McCrae, confirming that Tom was pushing against the Popeyes' expansion into Ontario.

"And if Carlito won't do it? The second hit?" I ask, trying to think clearly despite being scared out of my mind.

"He won't refuse. It was an order. He could rise up quickly and be big with the Popeyes. Or he could end up in a ditch or hanging from a beam. This is his big moment."

I text Brenda again, call her again.

Nothing.

Brenda's been staying with her aunt since Trent's murder, but she told me yesterday that she planned to go back to the townhouse, which is no longer sealed off as a crime scene. She probably told Carlito the same thing.

If Carlito wants to kill her, all he has to do is wait for her there. The same place he killed her brother.

Brenda won't be afraid when she sees him: she might even smile and ask him how his trip was, and keep smiling right until he pulls out his gun.

Chapter

45

I'm driving like a maniac and there's still no answer when I try Brenda's cell phone.

My next call is to Bill. I kind of ran out on him without an explanation, and am sure he's wondering what's going on.

"You okay?" he says. "Where did you go?"

He clearly saw the panic on my face when I ran out—and now he'll be able to hear it in my voice. I'm past being able to hide what I'm feeling. "I need you to do me a favor. Call the police. It's really important." I try to think of what our coaches tell us about staying cool in a game. There's no room for panic in the Zone. Just do the job the way you know it should be done.

"Of course. What?"

His tone is totally businesslike, professional.

I give him the address of the townhouse and ask him to tell the police that there's a gunman there. I know they'll take it seriously if the call's from Bill, and that he'll know how to speed things up.

"You've seen a gunman?"

"No, but I will." I'm hoping I won't, but I can't take any chances.

I'm just a few minutes from the townhouse now. I try to call Brenda again.

Still nothing.

I pull up to the townhouse and what I fear most is what I see next: Carlito is standing outside on the lawn with Brenda, a smirk on his face and a gun in his right hand. The gun is close to his body and someone driving by might not even notice it, but I can see it all right. There's a little flash of light off the silver toe of one of his cowboy boots. Brenda's facing him, her palms extended and empty, like she's trying to reason with him.

I'm just in time to watch her die.

I can't do a thing except sit in the car and stare. If I rush them, Carlito will open fire. He just has to move one finger and the girl I love is gone from the earth forever.

Somehow Brenda looks composed, even calm. If I didn't know better, I'd swear I saw a slight smile cross her face.

All I can do is watch, frozen in a bad dream.

Since the moment I first saw her, I've had this feeling that there's more to Brenda than meets the eye, that she has some sort of special power or inner light or whatever you want to call it. I wonder if Carlito senses that too. He glances at me for an instant as I sit frozen in my seat. He looks smug, as though he's enjoying having an audience.

What follows is like some crazy, slow-motion ballet. Brenda glides to her left as her right hand pushes the barrel of Carlito's pistol away. It's a short, efficient move that looks effortless. I guess I'm seeing the results of all that Krav Maga training.

Brenda's in her own Zone now.

Her hands and arms wheel around in a couple of sharp, powerful movements. Then she glides away smoothly with the gun now in her hand and leveled at Carlito. I can barely believe what I'm seeing, but Carlito's right hand is in obvious pain and his face is a knot of fury. He cocks his right leg as if preparing to deliver a hard kick.

Next, I see her right leg shooting out to deliver three crisp shots to his groin. One would have done the job but she's not taking any chances. Carlito grunts in pain as he rolls into a fetal position.

Brenda doesn't look afraid or angry or confused or amused.

Just deadly serious.

It would be so easy for her to finish him off with the gun. I wouldn't blame her if she did. It's probably what I'd do. And I certainly wouldn't rat on her.

Long moments pass.

Nothing happens.

Chapter
46

Three Dodge Chargers and a police van are parked outside the townhouse. Brenda has just a few minutes to load all of her stuff into their trunks and move on, once again, to a place that's totally new. She's going into witness protection. According to the conversations going on around us, the trials for Trollop and Carlito could take a couple of years. The police still have other killers to catch, and it's definitely not safe around here. They won't tell me where she's going. She doesn't even know herself yet. She just has to leave—now.

Cops wearing shades watch the roadway, just in case.

Brenda smiles at me but it's a pained smile.

There's so much I want to say. Too much for any one conversation. Or two. Or twenty. Definitely too much for a rushed talk surrounded by strange cops.

"I'm tired of starting over," she says. Her voice is weary and flat. "It's taken me a long time to find a friend like you."

"How will we stay in touch?" I say.

"The moon," she replies.

Just when I thought I couldn't love her more, she goes and says something like that. She's not taking love away. She's moving somewhere safer. Somewhere better.

I haven't even kissed her yet but I couldn't feel more like we're a couple than I do right now.

This is a chance for her to get away from the biker life and back in school, somewhere far away, maybe under a new name. That's the best thing for her and I'll have to adapt. We can figure it out. There are all sorts of places under our moon for us to meet.

I imagine Brenda won't have too much to say about Jamie to the police. He wasn't in the meth trade. He didn't take part in the murders. She'll have to answer questions about Carlito, though. I can't imagine what it's like to let someone into your world—into your bed—only to have that person destroy everything you care about. I guess Mom could tell me a little about that; maybe someday I'll ask her to explain.

"Time to say good-bye," a cop says.

"Come back for the prom." I just blurt it out. It's a joke and she gets it.

"How could I resist?" she replies as she walks toward one of the police cars.

A cop grimaces.

"I'll start picking out my dress now," she says next.

"You'll need a spatula to get me off you."

The grimacing cop is smirking now. Another cop looks seriously pissed.

"Text me when you get wherever you end up, okay? Don't say where you are. Just how you are."

"I'll be following your football career on the Internet. Do me proud."

She's right outside the car now but not getting in just yet.

The half dozen cops around her are getting anxious, but she doesn't seem to care.

"Remember the moon," she says.

I'm trembling and don't really know what to say. I've run out of ways to pretend this isn't happening. I take one last look at Brenda before she gets into the back of the Charger. She looks even more like a goddess than when I saw her in Trollop's barn, under the Confederate flag, between the tub of beer on ice and the meth whore.

As I get into the Cruze, I'm thinking of how I'd love to disappear down the road with Brenda. I'd love to run far and fast and forever with her but I can't— not yet. It's time to go home and patch things up with Mom. There are things about Mom and the way she lives that bother me more than I can say, and the truth is that they probably always will. I still love her, though. Dad left her. Even Carlito left her. I won't. I'll head off to university to try to make a go of it in football next year, but I'll never really leave her or Jamie.

Jake's texted me and wants to get together later. I have a lot to tell him and I like the idea of hanging out, but right now is for family. He'll understand.

━◦━

Mom's a bit startled when I walk in the front door a couple hours later. She looks defensive and sad and ashamed. I don't know what to say, so I just give her a hug. We haven't really spoken since the night that creep was over. It's time for me to step up. If she says anything about that night, though, I'll puke.

Mom's shaking a little and if I hold her any longer she'll likely start crying so I let go.

With me is Jamie. That breaks the tension. Mom's smile is so pure and raw and vulnerable when she looks at him that I feel like crying myself. It's a good feeling, and it's been so long in coming.

"What are you standing around for?" Jamie says. "Let's get the barbie started!"

"Don't boss me," Mom replies, but I can tell she loves it. Her boys are back in the house, so things are already looking up.